The Manager

by Caroline Stellings

The Manager

by Caroline Stellings

Cape Breton University Press
Sydney, Nova Scotia, Canada

Cape Breton University Press recognizes the support of the Canada Council for the Arts Block Grants program, and the Province of Nova Scotia, through the Department of Communities, Culture and Heritage, for our publishing program. The author also acknowledges the support of an Ontario Arts Council Writers' Works in Progress grant. We are pleased to work in partnership with these bodies to develop and promote our cultural resources.

Cover: Cathy MacLean Design, Chéticamp, NS
Layout: Mike Hunter, Port Hawkesbury and Sydney, NS
First printed in Canada

Library and Archives Canada Cataloguing in Publication

Stellings, Caroline, 1961-, author
    The manager : a novel / Caroline Stellings.

ISBN 978-1-927492-47-5 (pbk.)
ISBN 978-1-9274492-48-2 (web pdf.)
ISBN 978-1-927492-49-9 (epub.)
ISBN 978-1-927492-50-5 (mobi.)

    I. Title.

PS8587.T4448M35 2013   jC813'.6   C2013-903769-1

Cape Breton University Press
PO Box 5300, Sydney, NS B1P 6L2 Canada
www.cbupress.ca

For Joe

PROLOGUE

If Steinbeck's Cannery Row *is "a poem, a stink, a grating noise, a quality of light, a tone, a habit, a nostalgia and a dream," then Sydney's Whitney Pier is a tar pond, a coke oven, a million tons of contaminated soil, a broken field of black rubble and wild grass, a yellow mountain of pure sulphur and a long line of underground pipes that carry the deadliest chemicals known to humanity. Instead of sardines and junk heaps and honky tonks, it's lobsters, toxic sludge and fiddle music.*

That's how my sister Tina began her English essay. It got worse from there.

I wouldn't have to search too far around here to find the kind of folks that lived in Monterey – the whores, pimps, gamblers and sons of bitches that Steinbeck describes. I'm not sure how many pimps and gamblers there are in Sydney, because they keep it under wraps. There are plenty of whores, though, and I do know of one bona fide son of a bitch. My father. He makes up for all of Steinbeck's put together.

I didn't get a chance to read the rest of it; she grabbed it out of my hand when I proposed toning it down a bit. Tina didn't believe in toning anything down, and my suggestion to do so only prompted her to scribble a bunch of stuff in the margin while mumbling something about naming the whores.

She's right about my father though.

He blames his disposition on the coal mines. But then my father blames *everything* on the coal mines. Doesn't matter that he smokes three packs of cigarettes a day, his wheezing is black lung, caused from the years he spent down there. My mother didn't die from pneumonia, it was living near coal mines that did it. Bad weather? The mines. And my sister's condition, it was caused by the mines too. That and the fact she was born on the ides of March.

My father's been out of the ground for a few years now. But his fear of the mines has become morbid. He's terrified of having to work in the colliery again, especially now that he's almost forty-three. His father was forty-three when he died in the Springhill disaster – the so-called bump, which was really an earthquake that took out seventy-four men – and his grandfather was killed in the Sydney Mines accident twenty years before that. Crushed in a wreckage of cars when the haulage cable snapped, two weeks before his forty-third birthday.

If his business failed, and it was just about to, it would be back into the ground for Dad. Deep under the Atlantic ocean, where he was sure to die from falling rocks, asphyxiation from gas, silicosis or being run over by a coal car. His only hope – the only one who could save him from an early grave – was a young boxer named Ryan Byrne. That's what he thought. But life had a trick up its sleeve. Not just for my father – for Tina, too.

CHAPTER ONE

Saint Patrick's Day, 1979

"Time!" hollered my father. "What do you think this is, Byrne, a dancing class?" He banged his fist into the heavy bag. "Snap out that jab, do you hear me? Harder … harder…." He swore a few times. "You're a weakling. I mean it – a weakling."

"Dad," I said, "I'm leaving now. I'll be—"

"From the shoulder … from the shoulder it has to come." His eyes stayed fixed on Ryan Byrne, his only shot in the professional light-heavyweight division. Win that title, and the gym thrives. Lose it, and it's game over.

"Okay, whatever," he said, shooing me away with his left hand like I was a fly.

My father's gym was on the ground floor of a two-storey yellow brick building in Whitney Pier, a neighbourhood in the industrial part of Sydney, and we lived above it – he, my sister and I. He'd trained plenty of boxers, but no real contenders, just a string of palookas. Tenth raters. So when Ryan Byrne came along, it changed everything. My father would have done anything to be his manager – it's the manager who matters in boxing – but the twenty-year-old already had one of those and wasn't interested in my father whatsoever. Still, if Byrne could make it to the top, our gym would be a going concern. Young men would be banging on the doors for training, and maybe one of them would be good enough to need a manager. That was my father's dream. That was Sandy MacKenzie's dream.

I looked out through the dusty plate glass to the store across the street and waved to Azalea Lester. She's Black, and not Irish, but she'd taped up so many four-leaf clovers on her door and window, all I could see was her hand waving back. On the seventeenth of March, everyone around the Pier, Irish or not, managed to find something green to wear and drank beer and talked about luck. Except for my father. The only luck he believed in was the bad kind.

I walked past two half-naked Italians, sparring with their reflections in the full-length mirror, their moves quick, almost mechanical. Other young men jumped rope – jump, jump, jump, stiff as boards – or strained at sit-ups on floor mats. In the ring, two fighters bounced on and off the quivering ropes. Behind them, the peanut bag went *smacka-smacka-smacka* like a machine gun. And in the middle of it all stood my sister Tina, slamming a medicine ball into a welterweight's stomach and hollering louder than our father.

"Not good enough. Gotta be twice that fast or they'll have you for lunch out there. And don't look at me like that. You're not working on combinations. You've been throwing one punch at a time. No good. Jab, jab, hook. Got it?"

Dan Campbell was a couple years older than Tina. He was a university student and loved boxing, but he wasn't likely to make it far professionally. Life had been decent to him, so he didn't have the required chip on his shoulder; he lacked that need-to-make-somebody-pay attitude that will take an ordinary fighter and turn him into a winner. To get to the top in this sport, you've got to have a cold-blooded killer instinct – you have to sense where the other guy is weak, then belt him into next week with an uppercut to the jaw.

Flyin' Ryan Byrne was a good fighter, all right. But he wasn't hungry enough either, at least not according to Tina. My father exploded at the suggestion, but I think inside he knew she was right. After all, Dad had boxed during the late fifties and early sixties, when Cape Breton was a breeding ground for champions. Back when young men from New Waterford and Sydney Mines and the Pier spent long days working underground or the mill and tried to fight their way out of the grind by entering the ring. They had their eyebrows torn off and their jaws broken, but they kept on fighting because they needed to.

Still, Byrne was good and had a chance at a title, so my father spent every minute on him; the amateurs, like Dan, were last on his list. He got around to them eventually, but more often than not, it was my sister who taped their hands, rubbed Vaseline on their faces and showed them how to duck and bob.

"Tina," I said, "I'm going now. I'll see you later."

"Yeah, okay." She tossed the ball against the wall. "Take a break," she told Dan, "and don't forget the water. Every drop of it. Do you hear me?"

"Yes, Boss," he replied, giving her a dirty look. Then he turned to me and winked. "How do you stand her?" He sauntered off, shaking his head and mopping his brow.

Tina liked Dan Campbell. A lot. Of course she'd never admit it. She just worked him hard and hollered at him all the time. I think if she'd been a normal girl, she would have used my perfume and maybe a bit of mascara on the nights he was training at the gym. She did wear her pink sweats, though, and always washed her hair.

"I wish you'd change your mind," I said, hoping she'd come with me to the dance at the high school. But I knew she wouldn't. It was hard enough to get her to attend classes let alone social events. She hated the teachers. She hated the students. She hated the classrooms. She probably even hated the janitor.

"I could stay home, you know," I mumbled. "Maybe we could watch a movie or something. I don't care that much about the dance."

Tina narrowed her eyes.

"Damn it all, Ellie. Why the … why would I want to go to a dance? You know I never dance. And you know why I never dance. And please, stop acting so guilty. You look like you just ate the last cupcake. For God's sake, go to the dance. Go, go, go. I'll survive it."

"Why … why don't you ask Dan to come with you?" I forced out the words, swallowed hard and took two steps backward.

"Oh, crap. That's such crap, Ellie, and you know it is." Acid spilled off every word. "I pity the poor bastard that winds up at a dance with me." She fired three left hooks into the bottom of the closest punching bag.

"Maybe Dan would *like* to go." Another two steps back.

Tina didn't reply.

"Well, he might," I said.

She spelled something out with her lips, and it wasn't very nice. Then she turned away from me. "Nobody wants to dance with a midget." She made it sound like touring the morgue or being boiled in oil.

A young flyweight walked past us, bleeding from the forehead. Tina pulled a role of white adhesive tape out of the first-aid cabinet and tossed it to him. "Keep your chin tucked in," she told him. "You're leaving yourself wide open."

My sister had just turned eighteen. She's a year older than me, but whereas I was going to graduate in a year, she had miles to go. Miles to go and she'd probably never get there. Part of it was her own fault, and part of it was having to miss classes when the pain got bad. Her legs and spine gave her a lot of trouble.

Tina suffers from achondroplasia, a genetic mutation otherwise known as dwarfism. She never uses the word dwarf or midget, unless she's really mad at someone. And while most people born with the condition refer to themselves as little people, Tina hates that label too. She says she's four feet tall, but the last time we checked she was three foot eleven and a half. Which isn't bad for a dwarf. And she is beautiful. Her long reddish-blonde hair and big blue eyes, if they were pasted onto a young woman of normal height, would turn heads. My sister turns heads all right, but for the wrong reason.

So I marched solemnly out the door, went to the dance (which was one long sweep of mediocrity), and reminded myself every third song or so that I did have a right to have fun, even though I wasn't having any. The music committee, which was made up of boys from the audio/visual club (all of whom were also in the chess club), chose songs with the predictability of cost accountants. By the time "Stairway to Heaven" finished off the night, the girls were slumped over their boyfriends like seaweed on a rock, and I was ready to go home.

Anyway, I was glad Tina didn't come; whoever put up the decorations had an obvious penchant for paper leprechauns – they were glued to the walls, strung from the ceiling, used as centrepieces for every table and even stuck on the washroom doors. And if there was anything my sister hated more than teachers, it was leprechauns.

CHAPTER TWO

Living over a gym and surrounded constantly by men and the smell of sweat, Tina and I were used to all kinds of unsavoury things. We were accustomed to spit buckets and unflushed toilets and language that would make a sailor blush. We'd shared our meals with shady managers and crooked promoters, men with mashed-in faces whose eyes shifted back and forth like a metronome when you asked them to pass the ketchup. So when Tina told me she'd met a big shot from the world of boxing while I was at the dance, I kept on brushing my teeth and didn't pay much attention.

When she said it was Mickey O'Shea who had come by, the toothbrush fell out of my hand and bounced right out of the sink.

O'Shea, a racketeer from the west end of Montréal and kingpin of the Irish mob, made Al Capone look like Winnie the Pooh. I'd read about how he fenced stolen jewelry and brokered liquor and laundered money. And I knew that he fixed boxing matches in Montréal and Boston. But those activities were just hobbies for O'Shea. The big bucks were in illicit drugs. And the newspapers were rife with pieces about guys who got on O'Shea's bad side and ended up at the bottom of the St. Lawrence chained to a block of concrete.

I pictured him in a pinstriped suit and fedora, with thin yellow lips and a cigar hanging from one side of his down-turned mouth. Beside him, I saw two henchmen with close-set eyes and a gorgeous blonde who, when she removed her fur coat, looked underdressed for the swimming pool. I figured he had slammed through our front door, said "Outta my way, sister," when Tina asked for his autograph (since I know she's fascinated by organized crime), then held a gun to my father's head and told him there was no point in arguing, Ryan Byrne was boxing for the mob now.

"Don't be stupid," said Tina, snipping off the strands of my imagination like spaghetti between her teeth. "You've been watching those crap gangster movies again." Although she did admit that when O'Shea sat down, she noticed a handgun in an ankle holster. And it was indeed Ryan Byrne he'd come to watch.

"Mickey had on a dark blue cashmere sweater and jeans," she said casually. She pulled down her bed sheets and climbed in.

"Mickey?" I said. "You called him Mickey?"

"Not until we'd had a couple of beers."

"Beer?" I said. "You drank beer with a mobster?"

"I always have beer on St. Patrick's." She shut out the light. "They dye it green."

O'Shea's favourite colour, I thought. *The colour of money.*

"You went to the pub?" I turned the lamp back on. "And they didn't ask for ID?"

Tina looked at me with half-shut cobra eyes.

"You know why I don't get asked for ID don't you, El-lie? Waitresses are *afraid* to ask my age. They can't decide if I'm eleven or thirty-five."

"Oh, Tina," I sighed. "Come on, tell me more about O'Shea."

"He wanted to get a bite to eat. So what." She clicked the light off again, this time decisively. "Nobody else would go with him, so I offered. Besides, they have a great pool table over there." She grinned. "And I won twenty bucks."

I turned the light back on. "I can't believe Dad let you go."

Tina rolled over to face me. "Sandy doesn't give a damn what I do." She got out of bed, grabbed a shirt and unscrewed the hot light bulb. Then she stuck it in her bedside drawer and slammed it shut. Moonlight streamed through the window behind her.

"What did you talk about?" I asked. Really I wanted to know if he paid the waitress with a crisp fifty.

"Boxing," she replied.

"What else?"

"What else is there?"

I never understood what Tina saw in boxing. I kept thinking that one day, the magic of two men pummelling each other in the face would be revealed to me all of a sudden, like the contents of a letter written in lemon juice then held over a candle. But my sister was just as mystified when, on the first day of every month, I raced over to Azalea's and grabbed the new issue of *Seventeen* magazine out of her hand before she could put it on the shelf. Even more than leprechauns and teachers, Tina hated the articles in *Seventeen* – stuff like "Ex-boyfriends: Can You Still be Friends?," "What You Can Tell From Your Boyfriend's Palm," and "How to Make a Macramé Purse in One Afternoon." She said it was crap.

Tina preferred worn-out, filthy old copies of *The Ring* that had been passed around by every guy in the gym and read on buses, on lunch counters and on toilets. They'd been used as place mats under chili (you could tell from the stuck-on kidney beans), folded into a tube to be used as a megaphone during training and had big holes in them where somebody had torn out ads for muscle-boosting vitamins or cures for balding. To me, every cover looked the same: some man, naked from the waist, holding up his fists and looking like you'd just insulted his mother. Tina said it was the "bible of boxing" and besides, where else could you find articles on Joe Louis, Rocky Marciano and the Sugar Rays – Robinson and Leonard. I said it was no way to treat a bible.

Part of the reason why Tina didn't buy magazines and satisfied herself with these beat-up copies was because she was trying to save money. The pittance of an allowance our father gave us had to be used for clothes, so anything extra we had to earn ourselves. The two of us delivered newspapers, and we helped Azalea in the store whenever she asked us. I liked working for Azalea – and I wanted the money, too – but more often than not, I let Tina have the job because she needed it more than I did. And even though I strongly doubted she'd ever have enough saved, she remained firm in her conviction that one day she would be able to afford the surgery that was going to make her taller.

It was called the Ilizarov procedure, after a Russian physician. I didn't know who this Dr. Ilizarov was or from what school of masochism he graduated, but the whole thing sounded barbaric to me.

The procedure wasn't being performed in Canada yet, but in Boston, researchers had begun trials at a medical centre associated with Harvard University. It was Dan Campbell who suggested it to Tina in the first place; his uncle was working with a team of orthopedic surgeons trying to perfect the technique. But there was no way our father would pay for it, so all Tina could do was hope that one day she'd win the lottery or find buried treasure.

My sister couldn't be cajoled into seeing her life in a positive way – she resented being a dwarf. And hers was not a feeble little stick-out-your-tongue sort of resentment, but a deep-seated, I'll-make-you-and-everyone-I-know-miserable-because-I'm-miserable kind of bitterness. And there was nothing I could do to change her mind.

I tried to talk her out of the Ilizarov procedure, but trying to talk my sister out of anything was like trying to swim at the edge of a whirlpool. Probably the longest series of operations ever devised, the technique required using a saw to cut through the bone and screws that are turned every day while new tissue grows and a horrible frame worn on the limbs and an endless period of recovery. I couldn't stand the thought of my sister's limbs being cut like that and the excruciating pain that must be the result.

She told me that physical pain, no matter how much agony it entailed, was only temporary. I guess what she was really trying to say was that the other kind was endless.

"Tina?"

"Oh, for God's sake, Ellie, go to sleep," she snapped.

"What was it like, drinking beer with Mickey O'Shea?" I propped myself up on my elbow.

She rolled over to face me.

"If I tell you, will you shut up?"

I nodded my head.

"It's like this. We're both used to being gawked at every time we walk in a restaurant, every time we cross the street – hell, we can't even buy a pack of gum without somebody looking over their shoulder. So we agreed that it was nice, for a change, to imagine it was the other person that everyone was staring at."

CHAPTER THREE

By the time June rolled around, I had long since put O'Shea and the evil Dr. Sawbones out of my mind, having no idea that the two of them would soon be back to haunt me. I passed all my final exams and even tried to get Tina to attempt a few herself, but she refused, and Tina making up her mind was a process similar to pouring cement. She said she didn't want to. Said she didn't want to listen to teachers berate her for missing classes. Said she didn't want to be asked, "Where've you *been*?" and "Are you *okay*?" by well-meaning fellow students who, in Tina's words, were so enchanted with themselves for being nice to her, they floated a foot off the ground and left a trail of light wherever they went. She preferred the artless, uncaring ones from smoker's corner who laughed when she walked by. At least she could tell them to go to hell.

School was, for me, a chance to get away from the mouthpieces, gym equipment and B.O. that turned up everywhere in our apartment. Once, when I found a protective cup in our freezer beside the waffles and asked Tina what the heck that was all about, she squinted her eyes and shook her head in disbelief at the stupidity of my question, like I had just asked her why the frozen beans were in there. (It turned out to be an old trick to get a boxer moving when he first stepped into the ring.)

So when classes finished for the year, and the best respite I could hope for was the occasional moment of peace at Azalea's, the prospect of two long months of nothing but boxers and boxing was a sobering one. Which explains why I didn't put up much of an argument when presented with a golden ticket out of the Pier.

It was early in July when everything was set into motion. I'd put our supper in the oven and gone down to the gym to see if my sister would come to the store with me for a soda. But it was one of those rare occasions when my father was busy with the amateurs, so Tina had a chance to try coaching Flyin' Ryan, and nothing – fire, flood or earthquake – would get her to move.

"Byrne!" she hollered. "Keep your toes in. And you're forgetting what I told you – as a southpaw, it's got to work for you, not against you. I don't care what Sandy said. You've got to keep your strong arm for defence right from the get-go. And you've got to stay inside for the upper-cut. An uppercut from outside loses its power. You know that."

"Yeah." He ignored my sister, jumped back into the ring and continued sparring with the other boxer.

"What do you want?" Tina asked me, but her eyes were on Byrne. "No, no, no," she said. "You keep letting your right shoulder drop every time, Byrne. And when you're out there with a real contender, that's the opening he'll be looking for, believe me. Do you want to be drinking your meals out of a straw for six weeks? You drop that shoulder to throw an uppercut, and you'll be taking a left hook to the jaw."

"Do you want to go to Azalea's for a pop?"

"Not now, Ellie," she said through gritted teeth. "Byrne, I'm telling you, if you stay on the outside, he will see that uppercut coming. Your straight right jab can come from a distance, but—"

"What the hell are you telling him now?" My father stormed over to Tina and blew his whistle so loud he stopped every boxer in the gym and every car in the city. "I've warned you already about giving Byrne advice. He only needs one trainer and that is *not you*."

"You're teaching him the fancy moves, but you're forgetting the obvious," blurted Tina, her eyes raging and her face red with anger. "This business about waiting until the second round to reveal he's a lefty is crap, Sandy. It's a gimmick. And if you don't get Byrne to keep on the inside, he'll never make it to a national title. Never."

"And how many rounds have you gone in the ring?"

I'd hoped that Ryan Byrne would have stood up for Tina. Said something – anything. But as usual, he left my sister in the dust. I don't know why she wanted to be bothered with him, and I wasn't going to hang around and watch her be dismissed like that, so I headed across the road, leaving my father and Tina to duke it out, as usual.

"Hi, Azalea," I muttered, closing the door behind me. She had her radio tuned to a jazz station and turned it down when I came in.

"What's wrong? The two of them at it again?"

I took a cola from the refrigerator and checked my pocket for change.

"It's on the house," said Azalea. "That is if you'll sit a spell and tell me what's going on."

She opened two pops, and we sat down outside on the step. The skinny ash trees that grew up on each side of the store cast long shadows in the late afternoon sun, but the concrete felt warm under my legs. Cars passed by us, leaving dusty clouds that lazily drifted past.

"We could use some rain," said Azalea, looking up at the pale blue sky like she was waiting for it to start any time.

I realized I hadn't answered her question.

"My father and Tina can't agree about Ryan Byrne."

"Oh, I see." She took several sips of pop. "Well, I won't take sides, that's for sure, but your daddy, now he was quite a boxer himself back in the day. Must know something."

"Ever see him fight?"

"I sure did. Many times. I didn't get down to the matches in Halifax, but when my boys were young, I took them to every fight around here. And this was the place to be for boxing twenty years ago. Your daddy fought at the old Venetian Gardens, before it burned down, and in New Waterford and right here in the Pier."

"That must have been soon after he moved up from Springhill, with my mother."

"Yes, I guess it was. He was working in the Glace Bay mine then, and boxing every chance he could get." She smiled. "Oh, your father was exciting to watch. Most of his opponents couldn't last three rounds with him. Everyone thought he'd go straight to the top, but then...." Her expression changed.

"Yeah, I know. He injured his hand somehow."

"Shattered every bone. Never fought again." Azalea looked across the road to the gym. Then back up at the sky. "In 1963, it was. Just after your mother—"

"After she died?"

"Yes, Ellie." She took another sip of her cola, then poured a few drops out for a tiny ant that crawled over the step beside her. "You know, you look more like her every day."

"That's what my father told me," I said, and she put her arm around my back. I loved talking to Azalea, and I think she liked having me around, especially since her daughter didn't live in Sydney.

"Is Bonita coming home for the summer?" I asked. Azalea had four children, and Bonita, the only girl, was the eldest in the family. She taught school in Truro, and I was hoping to ask her about becoming a teacher myself.

"She'll be here tomorrow. She's going to spend a few days with me, then she's driving down through the New England states. Wants to visit the historical sights. You know Bonita."

"Are you going with her?"

"No, Ellie," replied Azalea. "I'd like to, but I can't leave the store for that long of a time." She pointed across the road at Tina who was heading our way. "Here comes your sister now."

Azalea went inside to fetch her a pop.

"Don't say a word, Ellie, I'm not in the mood." Tina plunked herself down beside me and buried her face in her hands. "God, this step is hot." She rubbed the underside of her thighs.

"Here you go," said Azalea, handing her the soda as the screen door closed behind her. "That'll cool you off."

Tina reached for the bottle and was about to thank Azalea when Dan Campbell pulled up beside the gas pump, just a few yards away from where we sat.

Tina jumped when she saw him. She looked like a kid who had been caught with a cigarette burning between her fingers. She started shoving her hair behind her ears. Then she tried to stretch her top down over her knees.

"Hey, Tina," said Dan. "And Ellie and Mrs. Lester. How are you ladies doing today?"

While Azalea and I chatted with him, I watched Tina from the corner of my eye. Without getting up, she slowly pulled a newspaper out of the stand next to her, then (when she thought nobody was looking) draped it over her lap.

I knew why. She wasn't expecting Dan to be around that afternoon, and she was wearing shorts. She didn't want him to see her legs.

"Tina," said Dan, leaning against the side of his car, "I have got the most unbelievable news. Unbelievable."

"Going to fight in the amateur bout in New Glasgow?" She looked up at him, shading her eyes with the back of one hand while holding the newspaper down with the other.

"No. It's better than that."

"Well, what is it?" I asked.

He turned to Tina.

"I told my Uncle Seamus all about you and he wants to meet you. If you fit the criteria for the study – and he thinks you will – he and his team will perform the operation. Gratis. Even the months you have to stay in the hospital will be free of charge. Free of charge!"

He sounded like he was trying to sell her a Veg-o-matic or sign her up for a correspondence course.

Tina said nothing.

I said nothing.

Azalea asked him what the devil he was talking about.

"The Ilizarov procedure. For limb lengthening. They're going to make Tina ... well, you know, they can increase her height. Fix her proportions. All she has to do is get herself to Boston." He looked at Tina again. "You can get to Boston, can't you?"

My sister had a glassy stare. It appeared to be a weird blend of embarrassment, indignation and fear.

I had a million thoughts in my head and couldn't get my lips around any one of them. Thank God for Azalea.

"Oh," she said, horrified at the suggestion, "that's ridiculous. Nobody goes under the knife that doesn't have to." She picked up the empty bottles and stood up. For a minute, I thought she was going to start throwing them at him. "Tina's a beautiful and healthy young woman. She doesn't need no fancy doctors changing her around."

"Tina wants to be made taller," said Dan. "Don't you, Tina?"

Tina nodded her head, sort of. But it was not up and down, nor was it from side to side. It was on a diagonal.

"Is it dangerous?" Azalea asked Dan.

He thought about it for a minute and then, with all the warmth of a Victorian spinster, replied, "There are risks with any operation. It's worth it for her to feel better about herself."

You mean you'll feel better about her, I thought.

"We'll talk later," he said, looking at Tina. He opened his car door and climbed in. "It's the opportunity of a life-time. Do you know how many people are trying to get a place in this trial?" He sped off in his two-seater like it was a white stallion. It's a wonder he didn't shout, "Hi-ho, Silver! Away!"

And Tina? She said nothing. Absolutely nothing.

When I tried to get her to respond, she just sat there, so pale and lifeless she looked like I'd just helped her out of a coffin.

Azalea put a hand on her shoulder, then went inside.

The newspaper dropped off Tina's knees.

"Well," I muttered, "Dan certainly cares about you. That's for sure."

God, I thought, *that sounded bad*. But I couldn't think of anything else to say.

Tina took a chunk of broken concrete and smashed it into a million pieces.

"Cares about me?" she snarled. "I'm so glad he 'cares' about me."

"What's wrong with that?"

"Nothing wrong with being cared for, Ellie. Noth-ing wrong at all." She reached for another piece of stone. "If you're a pet lizard or a great aunt." She stood up and started across the street.

And then I got it. I understood. Tina wasn't interest-ed in Dan's concern.

Tina wanted to be loved.

CHAPTER FOUR

Tina didn't mention Boston again and neither did I. I kept to myself for a couple of days, spending the long hours reading and looking out the window to see if Bonita Lester was around. Tina did what she always does: she boiled mouthpieces to fit the amateurs (pros like Ryan Byrne had theirs custom made by a dentist), brewed up her secret special salve (supposed to be a miracle styptic that stops bleeding instantly) and stood on top of a crate with two huge red training mitts on her hands, hollering at the young trainees to hit the bull's eye or she'd hit them.

I didn't care if she wanted to wear those big stupid gloves (even if, with her diminutive stature, she resembled a lobster) and I didn't care if she cooked mouthpieces (although I wished she wouldn't use our spaghetti pot to do so). But whenever it came time to whip up a batch of her miracle styptic, I prepared myself not only for the huge cleanup of the kitchen that would follow, but also for her cloak-and-dagger antics. Upon returning from the drug store with a brown paper bag full of unmarked tinctures, she would proceed to push two or three chairs against the kitchen door and draw the curtains before beginning her work.

I often listened from the hall and could hear her dragging the stepladder from one side of the room to the other so she could reach the cupboards, occasionally swearing when she burned herself on the stove and counting out one quarter teaspoon of this and two droppers full of that. What this and that were, I never did find out, although it wasn't from lack of trying. Once I even resorted to putting on sunglasses and a big hat and hiding in the pharmacy, in an attempt to hear what mysterious ingredients she was procuring from the druggist. (I was promptly taken aside by a clerk with crusty eyes who, in a low throbbing voice, filled me in on the various kinds of contraceptives they had in stock and how they should be used.)

To this day, Tina refuses to give up her recipe, and just like any 15th-century alchemist worth his salt, she's committed the constituents, the amounts and the cooking time to memory so that it won't be until she's been read the last rites that she will reveal what's in this magic styptic. Which explains why, when she had finally perfected her formula – when this mixture of herbal tinctures was able to stop the blood gushing from even the most stubborn laceration – she expected my father to jump for joy. A boxer with blood running into his eyes isn't going to last long in the ring, for three reasons: he won't be able to see a thing, the ringside physician will likely make him stop fighting (and his opponent will win by a technical knockout) and, since boxers aren't too far off vampires when it comes to their thirst for blood, the other guy is going to do everything he can to reopen the wound. This is why the cut man, who cleans up the bloody mess between rounds, is so crucial to the sport. And this is why Tina was so excited to unveil her elixir and test it out in the gym.

She crashed through the kitchen door with a jar of goo in one hand and the bag of vials in the other, told me the kitchen was a bit messy – the "bit messy" entailed a half dozen dirty pots and pans, three funnels stuck with wax, two sieves stained green and enough dirty tea towels to fill the washing machine – then ran downstairs, holding out her forearm where (again, like any good alchemist) she'd tried it out a few times by pricking herself with a pin.

I followed Tina to the gym to see if the stuff worked. Wasting no time, she pulled our father aside and insisted he try it on Byrne the next time he got cut, which was every hour or so, usually from a lace on his sparring partner's glove.

"Not now, Tina." Our father turned his back on her. "I'm busy."

"He's a bleeder, Sandy, and that's what's going to bring him down, I'm telling you." She looked at Flyin' Ryan. "Well, you almost lost that fight at Glace Bay because the cut man couldn't get your eyebrow to stop. Right? And the next time you're in a title match, I guarantee your opponent will head straight for it, and if the bleeding doesn't take you out, the ringside physician will."

"No thank you," said Byrne superciliously. "My manager looks after everything."

"Tina," snapped my father, "I don't have time to deal with this. Can't you find something else to do?"

"Maybe the salve will work," I said to Byrne, but he just shrugged his shoulders and continued punching the numbered bag, which, to my mind, had more brains than he did.

Tina watched him for a minute. Then she held up her hand.

"Ryan, let me ask you something," she said, and he dropped his arms. "You're fighting for the Eastern Canadian light-heavyweight championship soon, right?"

He nodded.

"Then you plan on taking a national title and after that, a North American one?"

"You know that," said Byrne, tapping his gloves together, like he'd already won.

"My God, girl," said my father. "We haven't got all day."

"You're a good fighter, and you don't throw junk," declared Tina. "But being technically correct is one thing and winning is another. If I was your manager—"

"Which you are not," said my father.

"If I was your manager, or even your *trainer*," said Tina, casting a combative glance at my father, "I would be a whole lot more concerned about your thin skin than having you memorize combinations on this dummy." She punched it, and it swung back at her.

My father coughed up a laugh. "Give it up, kid. Go and make yourself useful someplace, will you?"

Useful. I knew that was going to do it. If it's true that defeat is a lot of little things, I figured that one six-letter word was the final push that would send my sister over the brink. And it did.

"Useful?" cried Tina. "All I ever do is make myself useful. I help you every day in this stupid gym."

"She does," I muttered.

"Okay, Sandy," she declared, "I'm getting the hell out of this dump. And I'm not coming back." She looked at Byrne. "So you're not interested in this?" she asked him, holding out the jar of goo.

He didn't even answer her that time. Just turned away.

Arrogant jerk, I thought.

Tina looked around the room, and no one was sparring. No one was doing sit-ups. No one was skipping rope. All the young men were listening. Some of them were grinning. Not one of them had the guts to stand up for Tina and tell Sandy how important she was to the gym. How important she was to them. I wished Dan was there. Maybe he would have.

Her face went red again, but this time it wasn't from anger – it was utter humiliation, and she took off. The door slammed behind her. My father carried on with Byrne like nothing had happened.

"You insulted her, Dad," I said, but he didn't hear me.

I followed Tina outside. She was leaning with both hands against the side of a tree and there were tears in her eyes. She had plenty to cry about but rarely did, so I was taken aback when I realized how upset she really was.

"Let's go over to Azalea's and get a cone or something," I said, fishing in my pocket to be sure I had enough change.

"I'm leaving, Ellie."

"What?"

"I'm leaving."

Tina had threatened to check out of Whitney Pier many times, so I didn't take her seriously, although this time there was something different about her voice. It was quiet. Too quiet.

"Come on," I insisted. "Let's go to the store."

Tina walked next to me and stared straight ahead; when we got there, she sat herself down on the step, told me she wasn't the least bit interested in ice cream and insisted that I find out if Bonita was home yet.

She was, and she and Azalea joined us outside.

After a round of hugs and how-have-you-beens, the four of us perched ourselves across the front steps like a row of pigeons. Bonita was one of those women who embarked on every conversation with the vivacity of a kid carrying new ice skates and could slide smoothly from sociopolitical issues like the economic liberty of women and the oil crisis in the Middle East to a recipe for raspberry muffins. I asked her about being a teacher and about her upcoming trip through the New England states.

Tina was quiet throughout it all, but I could tell by the way she kept rubbing her tongue against her top row of teeth that she was preparing herself for something. While the seagulls swooped and hollered over our heads, and cars raced by, and we passed around topics such as designer jeans and the weather like they were salted peanuts, my sister said nothing. Then, when there was a three second lull – somewhere between how many miles to the gallon you get on the highway and the vacuum cleaner salesman with large transparent ears who'd asked Bonita to the movies – Tina decided to drop the bomb.

"Bonita?" she said softly, as if she was about to ask her where she'd bought her skirt or where she'd ever managed to find such a pretty purse.

"Yeah Tina?"

"When are you leaving for the States?"

"Tomorrow." Bonita leaned back and rested both elbows on the step behind her.

"Tomorrow?" asked Azalea. "Why so soon? Can't you stay a few more days?"

"Oh, Mama." She reached out for her mother's hand. "I'll be back by the middle of August and we can spend a couple of weeks together, okay?"

Azalea smiled. "I guess I don't have much choice, now do I."

"Are you going as far as Boston?" Tina asked. Her eyes were focused on Bonita's so intensely I expected she could learn the answer by reading her mind.

"Yes, I am, and—"

"I'd like to come along, if you have room. I will pay you for the gas and any other expenses, and—"

"No!" hollered Azalea. "No, Bonita. Tell her no."

"Well ... why not?" Bonita turned to me. "What's going on?"

"Tina needs to get to Boston, to a medical centre at Harvard, because—"

"Because Tina is a dwarf," said my sister. "And because Tina is sick of being a dwarf and because Tina is sick of being treated like crap." She stood up. "Look, Bonita, can I come with you to Boston or not?"

Azalea shook her head and went inside. I followed.

"You can't let her get those operations," Azalea insisted. "Those doctors are just looking for a guinea pig."

"There's no way to stop her. She's eighteen now, so she can do what she wants."

Azalea held a finger to her mouth and stood next to the screen door. She signalled me to come quietly.

We listened to Bonita and Tina and although I felt like we were peering into someone's medicine cabinet, it didn't stop me from eavesdropping. At first, I thought their conversation might turn out to be a boring one, especially when Bonita started into Machiavelli and whether or not the end justifies the means. Soon, however, I was riveted to the wall.

"I know what it's like to face discrimination on a daily basis, believe me," said Bonita. "Growing up Black was never easy, and trying to get a decent teaching position was no walk in the park either." She sighed. "But I don't think I'd subject myself to a series of operations to change it."

"That's because you can reach the pay phone," declared Tina, breaking a small twig into pieces. "And you don't have to ask someone to push the elevator button for you."

"No."

"Have you ever been called…." Tina had trouble repeating the adjective she'd had hurled at her a hundred times. "Have you ever been called a retard?"

"No," said Bonita. "I haven't."

"And when it comes to job opportunities, you aren't limited to babysitting for the rest of your life or joining a travelling circus."

Bonita didn't reply at first. Then she asked Tina if she could be ready by noon.

CHAPTER FIVE

The next morning I found my father slumped over the breakfast table with a newspaper and coffee, a cigarette burning precariously close to his lips. Beside him sat a ledger for his bookkeeping, a couple of bank books and a pencil that was chewed down to a stump. I had to pry a bank statement out of his hands to get him to eat the special French toast I'd prepared. I wanted him to have an open mind when Tina came down to tell him she was going away. For a long time.

He poured syrup until it flowed to the edge of the plate. One drip went over the side.

"Dad?"

"What is it?"

Before I'd found the courage to answer, I heard a knock downstairs at the front entrance to the gym.

"Beat it," hollered my father. "We don't open before noon."

"I'll see who it is," I said, scrambling down the front staircase.

It was Dan Campbell.

"You're early," I said, unlocking the door. "Tina hasn't even told my father yet."

"I promised my girlfriend I'd drive her out of town this morning."

Girlfriend.

"Girlfriend?" My hands got clammy and my stomach flipped over. All this time I thought, maybe, he liked Tina. "I didn't know you had a girlfriend. I thought...."

"What?"

"Forget it."

Since Dan's knowledge of human emotion could be put through the eye of a needle, I didn't have much hope in educating him in the art of dealing with people's feelings.

"After Tina called last night, I set things up with Uncle Seamus. I didn't give him an exact arrival date, because Tina said Bonita Lester wants to do a bit of sightseeing on the way to Boston. He's fine with that." He handed me a map and directions to the hospital. "So he'll be ready for you two when you get there."

"We two?"

"Tina said you were going with her."

"She did?"

Dan looked at his watch. "I'm running late. Tell Tina good luck, okay?"

Good luck? That's it? How could I tell Tina that Dan isn't interested in her? Isn't it because of him she's getting her limbs sawed in half?

"Tina," I said, once back upstairs in our room, "Dan left this map and directions."

Without even looking at it, she folded it up into a wad and stuffed it into her purse.

"He thinks I'm going with you."

"Well, aren't you?" said Tina. "And why haven't you packed yet? Bonita will be ready to leave in a couple of hours."

"I can't stay in Boston for a year. I have to go back to school in September."

"Don't you want to get out of the Pier for a couple months? Bonita said once I'm settled in Boston, you can come home with her." She pushed down on the clothes in her suitcase, then tried to force it shut. "I don't care. Do what you want."

Out of the Pier for a couple months. The words were dripping with milk and honey.

"Oh, damn this thing," said Tina. Then she pulled out a pair of jeans and tossed them onto the floor. I noticed she had room for that enormous jar of salve.

"Why are you bringing that?" I asked.

"I'm not leaving it here. That's for sure."

"Tina," I said bravely, "there's something I need to tell you."

"Can't it wait?" said Tina. "I've got Sandy to deal with." Not exactly thrilled with my role as a bottomless pit of bad news, I was happy to wait. As it turned out, it was a good thing I did.

—

"I've decided to go to Boston, Sandy," said Tina, her eyes as cheerful as a wet rag. "You don't want me here anyway."

"I didn't say that."

"You might as well have."

"Have it your way then."

"Okay."

"Okay."

I picked up my father's plate and set it in the sink. Then I swung around to face him.

"Can I go too? Just for a few weeks?"

"No."

"I'll come back with Bonita."

"NO."

"Jesus Christ, Sandy, can't you let the girl have a life?" She pushed one of the chairs hard against the kitchen table so it crashed beside him. "It's one thing to be miserable with me all the time. Hell, you make me feel like a package that's been left on the wrong porch. Maybe you think I don't have much of a life to ruin. But Ellie has a chance. Don't wreck it for her."

He looked at me.

"Who's gonna make my meals?"

"Make your own meals," said Tina.

I thought about it for a minute. "I could ask Azalea to—"

"He can look after himself for a couple of weeks, Ellie," declared Tina. "Maybe he'll appreciate you when you get back." She gave the chair another push, this time a gratuitous one, and went back to our room.

My father lit another cigarette.

"I think Tina wants me there for moral support," I said.

"I think the whole thing is a stupid waste of time," he said.

"It doesn't matter what either one of you thinks," hollered Tina. "And by the way...." She came back into the kitchen. "Other than Dan Campbell and Azalea, nobody around here needs to know what I'm doing."

"What the hell am I supposed I tell them?" asked my father.

"Tell them I died. Tell them I'm going to take a stab at Mount Everest. Tell them whatever you want, I don't care."

Dad didn't see us off. He went downstairs to the gym and started repairing the ropes around the ring. I asked him if there was anything he wanted me to bring back from the States, but he shrugged and grunted something about not spending all my money.

—

Bonita gassed up her car, and what a car it was. A 1959 Thunderbird convertible in Brandywine Red. I'd always admired it but had never taken a close look. It had red seats with white insets, a dashboard that reflected light in every direction and fins! The car was twenty years old but didn't have a spot of rust on it. It looked like someone had driven it off the set of *American Graffiti*.

"I treat Brandy with tender loving care," said Bonita. "She was my daddy's, before he passed on."

"Brandy's in great shape," I said, admiring the whitewall tires.

"Oh, great shape," echoed Bonita. "She's going to need a new rad sometime, but other than that, she purrs like a kitten."

We loaded our things into the kitten's trunk, and I saw Tina glance over to the gym to see if our father was watching. He wasn't.

Azalea hugged each of us. Bonita took a container of coolant from the trunk, released the hood and filled up the rad, while Tina commandeered the front seat (claiming that if she sat in the rear, the only thing she'd see would be the back of my head.)

Azalea had a word with me alone.

"You're not going to let her go through with this, are you?" she asked, her eyes soft and sad.

"You know what my sister's like," I admitted. "But I will try."

"Good girl," she said, giving me another hug.

"Azalea?"

"Yes, dear?"

"Can you look in on my father every once in awhile? See that he has food in the fridge?"

"Yes, Ellie. I'll make sure he doesn't starve." She opened the car door for me, and I hopped in. "Don't worry yourself," she told me. "Have a good trip and bring me back some pictures, you hear?"

We all waved goodbye as we motored down the street. Bonita honked the horn a few times and turned on the radio. "Wheel in the Sky" played, and with the wind blowing through my hair, I felt pretty smug as the Pier disappeared gradually in the rear-view mirror. I wasn't just going on a trip, I was leaving the world of men and their fists behind me and watching as a whole new vista opened up. Before long, we were sailing down the highway and I couldn't have been happier.

And then came the tragic realization that my utopian state was nothing but a daydream and that Count Ilizarov was waiting at the end of that road, a smile on his face and a hacksaw in his hand.

CHAPTER SIX

We stopped near Antigonish at a roadside diner. Bonita had driven for a couple hours by then, and we were all ready for a snack and a chance to stretch our legs. The place was blue with smoke and had rows and rows of booths and round seats lining a counter that ran from one end of the building to the other. People shuffled in and out so quickly, the seats never cooled off, and every time someone in shorts got up to leave, it sounded like the peeling of cellophane from Tupperware as their thighs became unstuck from the leatherette.

Tina and I followed behind Bonita and looked for an empty booth, but the only one was at the far end. Every eye was on my sister – it was as if she had six or seven neon signs directed at her. Most folks pretended to be eating their fries, but a couple of kids laughed at her. The smacks they received from their mother didn't do much to help the situation – in fact it only made it worse, since it drew even more attention to my sister and forced the kids into defending their actions.

"But it's a little woman," said the one kid, and the other one nodded in agreement.

Clearly the waitress hadn't heard the remark and didn't realize that Tina was, in fact, a woman.

"Hello ladeez," she panted, pulling a pencil out from behind her ear. "I'm Ruby and I'll be your waitress today. Our specials are western sandwich with fries, toasted clubhouse with soup and salad or deep-fried shrimp and chips. Coffee's on the house and children under twelve eat for half price," she said with a faint smile while pointing her pencil at Tina.

Then she did a double take.

"Sawry," she added, handing us each a menu.

"I'll have a slice of lemon meringue pie," said Bonita, "and you girls have whatever you'd like. It's my treat."

Ruby suggested the shortcake, then apologized again.

"So, Mama says this Flyin' Ryan fellow is going to win some big titles," Bonita said, after Ruby'd slapped down some well-used flatware and left for the kitchen. "He's good, is he?"

"He's supposed to win the Eastern Canadian championship," I said. "If he does, it will mean more business for our father, and we won't lose the gym."

"I hope your daddy can stay in business," sighed Bonita. "The poor man's had enough trouble."

"Poor man?" bellowed Tina. "You're kidding me."

"Well, with his hand and everything. Having to quit like that, right before the fight for the British Empire crown." She took three serviettes out of the dispenser and passed them around.

"The British Empire title?" Tina squinted her eyes. "I didn't know he had a chance at that."

"He didn't tell you about it?" said Bonita. "You two were babies at the time, but I was there. The match was going to be in Sydney." She smiled. "Your father was the card, really. He was the draw."

Draw. Card. I thought I was getting away from all this boxing blab.

"Anyway," continued Bonita, "I just hope this Byrne wins a title or two."

"Never going to happen," declared Tina, leaning to the side so Ruby could stick a ginger ale in front of her.

"Will you be wanting anything else?" she asked, holding up her index finger at a table of impatient customers to get them to wait a minute. We shook our heads, and she ripped our bill off her pad, mumbled a few meaningless words about the weather, obviously in the hope of securing the tip she figured she'd already lost, then went on to the next booth.

"What do you mean, never going to happen?" I asked Tina. "I know Byrne's a jerk, but...."

"He hasn't got what it takes."

"He doesn't?"

"No, Ellie, he doesn't." She sucked up her ginger ale through a straw, then tilted the glass so she could get at the ice. After crushing it between her teeth and letting it fall back into the glass, she explained. "I'm not saying that Byrne isn't a good technical fighter, but that's not worth squat if he lands in the ring with a wildcat."

"My best friend Louise's husband manages a fighter like that." Bonita swallowed a big piece of pie. "This is delicious, by the way."

"What's his name?" asked Tina.

"Jesse Mankiller."

"Mankiller?" I asked.

"Oh yeah," said Tina. "I read something about him. What's his real name?" she asked.

"That is his real name," Bonita responded. "He's Cherokee on his father's side – Mankiller is a traditional Cherokee name – and his mother is Mi'kmaw." She took another bite. "He lives in Millbrook, the reservation near Truro, with his mother and sisters. Don't know what happened to his father." Then she grinned slowly from ear to ear. "Louise says his name should be womankiller, he's that handsome."

"And this guy's a contender, right?" asked Tina, more interested in his boxing skills than his good looks.

Some teenagers sat down next to us and smirked when they noticed my sister. She was about to gesture with a finger (and unlike Ruby, it wasn't her index finger), but I grabbed her wrist.

"Forget about it," I told her.

"Mankiller's good," Bonita explained, "but he's unpredictable. Moody. One minute he's going to take on the world, and then he turns on a dime and Paul can't deal with him."

"Paul?" I asked.

"Paul Holley, Louise's husband. He's betting everything he's got on this Jesse Mankiller. Says he's going to take the world title one day. If he can stop chasing after girls, that is."

"Mankiller hasn't ever lost a fight, has he," inquired Tina.

"I don't think so."

"I thought we were getting away from boxing," I said, in a whiny attempt to steer the conversation (not to mention my life) away from the ring.

Bonita got my drift, and from that point, she and I flitted back into the world of fashion and school teaching and the sort of topics that left my sister in the dust. She clammed up and said nothing for the rest of the afternoon.

It was almost six by the time we reached Truro. Bonita's little stucco cottage sat proudly at the end of a tree-lined side street. Surrounded by flowering bushes and shrubs and sporting freshly painted shutters in a cheery shade of yellow, her house was small but well-kept, immaculate. On the front porch sat wicker furniture with floral cushions that matched the shutters, and I thought to myself that one day, I was going to have such a pretty and feminine place to live.

"My God, your grass is perfect," chirped Tina, once she'd decided to talk again. "What do you do? Cut it blade by blade?"

Bonita laughed and opened the door for us. Her home was just as nice on the inside and smelled so much better than our place.

She told us to boil up a package of pasta while she got some sheets and made up the spare room. I searched around in the cupboards for canned sauce and Tina located a couple of pots, and somehow we managed to work together in the confines of the small kitchen without pulling each other's hair out.

Someone knocked on the front door; I answered it.

"Well, hello," said the visitors, an attractive Black couple with warm smiles. "Who are you?" asked the man.

"I'm Ellie, Bonita's friend."

"That you, Paul?" Bonita hollered from the back room. "Come on in. I'll be with you in a second."

"We'll wait on the porch," said the woman. "There's a good breeze out here right now." The two of them sat on the loveseat, and I took the chair, leaving Tina to carry on with the supper, a task for which a boll weevil was better equipped.

Paul and Louise Holley introduced themselves, then Bonita came out and joined us.

"I wish I could go with you," said Louise. "I'd love to see the New England states." She sighed. "But Paul's going to be away most of the summer, so I have to stay with the kids." Bonita told me they had three children, and the youngest was only six.

"Where are you going, Paul?" asked Bonita.

"I've got fights set up for Jesse Mankiller. We're starting in Halifax tomorrow night – the American promoter wants to see him in action. He's trying to generate some local interest because they're holding the U.S.–Northeast light heavyweight championship in Amherst this year. Win that one and it's on to Portland for the American title."

"Jesse's from the States," Louise explained.

"Anyway," continued Paul, "if he doesn't kiss the canvas in Maine, we're heading to Boston for the North American title."

"Kiss the canvas?" Bonita asked.

"Oh come on – you know what that means. A face-down knockout," answered Tina, whose nose had been pressed to the screen ever since the word fight was uttered.

"Who's this?" asked Louise, pulling open the door.

"My sister, Tina," I mumbled.

While the next round of introductions was taking place, I could smell something burning. I ran in and saved the sauce – barely. Tina came in behind me.

"Don't you dare tell them why I'm going to Boston," she hissed.

"You burned the supper."

"No I didn't."

"Well if it wasn't you, then who?"

"The stove did it."

"The stove did it?" I asked. "You know, you always used to say stuff like that. When we were little."

"I did?"

"Don't you remember, when you got that huge wad of gum stuck in your hair and it took Dad a week to get it out?"

Tina laughed. "You're right. I told him the bubble did it."

Bonita and Louise came inside to set the table. Paul had gone next door for a bottle of Chianti.

"I'm worried about him," said Louise.

"Worried about Paul?" asked Bonita. "What for?"

"I don't know. He's tired all the time. And yesterday he was short of breath. I know it's been hot lately, but...."

"Probably just anxiety over this new fighter of his." Bonita put a cloth napkin beside each plate.

"Maybe," said Louise. "I hope you're right."

Paul returned with the wine, and we all sat down to a plate of overcooked spaghetti and sauce that tasted a little bit like charcoal, but nobody seemed to mind.

Flowered cushions, cloth serviettes, the smell of potpourri instead of feet – it was paradise to me. The conversation was lively and I was truly enjoying myself. And then Satan, in the form of boxing, entered the Garden, and Tina and Paul spent the better part of an hour arguing over who'd had the most devastating punch in history. By the time they'd decided on Joe Frazier's left hook, I'd decided that pugilism, and everything it entails, had chosen to stalk me like a B-movie slasher and would track me down no matter how far I ran from Whitney Pier.

CHAPTER SEVEN

We pulled into the reservation in Paul Holley's station wagon. Kids ran around in various stages of undress, playing with rocks and sticks and pieces of plastic toys. Empty beer cans and gin bottles lined the dusty roads, and the homes were nothing but rusted trailers and shabby cabins. A few of the shacks were in better shape and had a new car or truck parked outside; Paul said some of the men had found jobs when a factory opened up nearby.

When a couple of boys kicked a soccer ball in front of us and we had to stop for a minute, I noticed two teenaged girls sitting on crates in front of a trailer. One of them was nursing a baby. I tried to look away – I didn't want her to see me staring – but she spotted me and smiled. I don't know why, but I was embarrassed and didn't smile back.

Tina, sitting next to Paul in the front seat, was too busy making plans for Jesse Mankiller's big fight in Halifax to notice anything.

"Do you think Mankiller has a chance against Mason Pitts?" she asked. "I hear he's good. Doesn't fall easily."

"I don't know. Until tonight, Jesse's been fighting undercard matches, and nobody's been able to take him down. He's only nineteen, but I think he's got the potential to go to the top in the professional circuit." Paul swung the car around a broken-down truck. "He's got crisp jabs, and he's fast."

"Can't wait to see this guy in the ring," said Tina.

The two of them went on and on, and I wished I hadn't come with them. But I didn't want to be in Bonita's hair all night; I figured that she would like some time to herself. So when Paul offered to take Tina and me to watch the fight in Halifax, I acquiesced. I figured a fight was the only thing that would get the Ilizarov procedure off Tina's mind – she didn't say anything, but it must have been haunting her. It was scaring the hell out of me. Anyway, I'd never been to the big city, so even if it meant spending a Saturday night watching boxers, at least I'd get to see Halifax.

Paul pulled up in front of a long, weather-beaten trailer. Actually, it was two trailers stuck together to make a square house. The siding was grey with red stripes, and the front door had fallen off and was propped up against the side. We parked the car and two kids ran over with their hands out. Paul handed them each a candy bar then knocked on a piece of plywood that was being used as a substitute door. Another piece of thicker plywood formed a ramp from the trailer to the ground.

A young girl pulled back the door.

"Hey, there," said Paul, "is your brother home?" The girl nodded and ran back inside.

A few seconds later, a young man appeared.

I knew he must be Jesse because not only was he the most handsome guy I'd ever seen in my life, he had the body of a boxer. Firm and fit. His long black hair was tied back into a ponytail. He wore nothing but a pair of sweat pants, and I started to shake.

He looked at me with piercing brown eyes. I shook even more. Then he looked at Tina – one of those long, slow looks – and made no attempt to disguise the fact that he noticed she was a dwarf.

"These are friends of mine, Tina and Ellie MacKenzie," said Paul. "They're coming with us to Halifax." He pointed at my sister. "Tina's quite an expert in boxing."

"Oh yeah." Jesse sounded like Paul had just told him that cabbages were on sale at the supermarket.

I don't think my sister had any conception of what was going to happen to her when she met Jesse. No, she was thinking like a boxing trainer, and it wasn't until she came within a foot of his gorgeous body that any female hormones left in her – any that had managed to stay afloat in the sea of testosterone she'd been swimming in from reading nothing but *The Ring* – came rushing to the surface, demanding to be recognized. Sure, she'd been around many young male boxers – we both had – but none of them came close to Jesse Mankiller.

Tina was speechless for a full minute and her eyes never left the ground. Her feet did, though. She slowly lifted her heels so she'd appear to be a couple inches taller.

Jesse moved aside and unceremoniously ushered us through the door. What was supposed to be the living room was long and narrow, and a woman in a wheelchair, with an afghan over her lap, nodded her head when we sat down on the couch. A couple of girls – the one who'd opened the door for us and another who was a bit younger – sat in front of her and were playing with a doll that had no hair.

"Beer?" asked Jesse.

Tina and I shook our heads to say no.

"Forget about beer," scolded Paul. Then he apologized. "I'm just getting a bit restless. I need you in top form in …," he looked at his watch, "about four hours from now." He raised an eyebrow. "You've been gettin' plenty of rest? Eating what I told you?"

Mankiller didn't answer.

"Got a goddamn headache," he complained, taking a bottle of aspirin out of a drawer in a cupboard beside him. He opened the jar.

"I wouldn't do that if I were you," warned Tina.

Jesse looked at Paul. "What's she talking about, Holley?"

"Thins the blood," she said. "If you get cut, we'll never stop the bleeding." She caught herself. "I mean, your cut man will never stop the bleeding."

The old Tina was back in business and for once, I was glad to see her. Okay, so I knew she was hiding behind her expertise because boxing was the only thing on earth that gave her confidence, but she needed it.

Mankiller ignored her and went to pop the aspirin in his mouth.

Paul stopped him. "She's absolutely right, Jesse. You've got to be clotting even more than cottage cheese tonight."

Sensing her vindication, Tina decided to throw in a few more of her ideas for good measure.

"And Paul," added Tina, "I'd limit the use of ammonia pellets if I were you. Maybe we could bring some vinegar instead, okay?" Now my sister was showing off a bit, but the fact she was a dwarf was the elephant in the room. How else could she deal with it?

"No ammonia bombs?" asked Paul.

Tina explained that while it was true that one sniff of those things is enough to jolt a dazed and staggering fighter back into the ring, ammonia increases blood pressure and therefore bleeding. My sister thought of everything.

"Got any vinegar?" Paul asked Jesse, who just shrugged his shoulders and walked away.

Paul leaned against the wall. He appeared short of breath and kept putting his hand over his chest.

"Are you okay?" I asked him. "Do you need water?"

"No, thanks, I'm fine. Just a bit hot." He sat down in a chair, but he didn't look fine to me.

I noticed that Jesse's mother hadn't said a word since we'd arrived, so I asked her if she was proud of her son and his excellent undefeated record. She smiled and nodded, but still didn't say anything.

Then I saw the crutches next to her wheelchair. I looked down to where her feet should be and there was only one. I could see that her leg had been amputated at the knee. Now there were two elephants in the room.

The older child spoke up. She'd been studying Tina for some time and had finally gotten up the nerve to ask the fateful question: "Are you an elf?"

Tina turned red, then white, then an odd shade of putty-grey.

"No," said Jesse, "now go take a nap, okay?" He led her by the hand, then picked up the younger girl and took them into the bedroom.

"But she looks like an elf," we heard the girl say from the next room. That was why Tina never wore green or anything with stripes.

Paul hollered that it was time to go, so we stood up. Jesse got his duffel bag and threw on a shirt.

"Just a minute," he said.

He went to the kitchen area, opened a fridge (it was half the size of an ordinary one and contained mostly beer and cheese) and pulled out a vial of milky liquid. Then he took a needle out of the cupboard, jammed it into the vial, tilted it up and measured out an exact amount, which he took to his mother.

"Insulin," whispered Paul. "Mrs. Mankiller is diabetic. That's how she lost her leg."

Just as we were getting into the station wagon, a girl came staggering to the trailer. She was about fifteen and had a sad, weary sort of expression. I figured the girl – Jesse called her Meryl – must be one of his sisters, because he gave her instructions about looking after their mother. Then he told her not to get drunk, despite the fact she was clearly three sheets to the wind. She stumbled up the ramp and pulled the plywood across the opening to the trailer. I promised myself at that very moment that I would never complain about my room over the gym again.

CHAPTER EIGHT

The Halifax Forum was a huge old place and smelled damp and musty as we made our way down the narrow halls. It was shabbier than I'd expected, with wooden planks over the ice and a ring that had seen better days.

Tina didn't care. As long as there was a ring in there someplace, it was heaven to her.

Paul complained that the marquee didn't make enough of Jesse Mankiller and seemed to favour his opponent, because the letters that spelled out MASON PITTS were much bigger.

Jesse said he didn't give a damn, but Paul said if they didn't bother to stick to what was in the contract regarding something like the sign, they were sure to try to screw him somewhere else.

"They're just out to unnerve him," Tina said. "Want him to panic a bit so their local boy has a better chance. That's what it is."

Jesse listened to what she said but didn't reply.

We were almost to the dressing room when Paul stopped us, gave us our ticket stubs so we could find our seats, and said he'd meet us at the front entrance once the fight was over.

"Don't you want me to tape his hands?" asked Tina. "Help him warm up?"

Jesse glared at Paul.

"Who's your cut man?" Tina barked. When they didn't answer instantly she realized they were taking one appointed by the promoter. "Oh, no!" she said. "That's ridiculous. How do you know they'll play fair?"

"Our budget doesn't allow for a cut man," said Paul. "Not yet, anyway."

"Well you won't know if the cut man is any good or not. You have to pace Mankiller. You have to keep an eye on Pitts, watch for mistakes. How can you be sure the cut man is on the level?" She shook her head in disgust. "I can do this for you. I can get my salve approved by the ringside physician in two seconds." She pulled it out of her purse. "Come on."

Jesse glared again.

"If you think bismuth and thromboplastin is enough, you're crazy," she gasped.

"Thanks, but I've got everything covered," said Paul.

"Okay, whatever," snapped Tina. Venom dripped out the side of her mouth.

I looked at my ticket. "Ringside!"

"Only place to be," said Paul.

A group of young men spotted Jesse and made stupid Indian war calls. He was about to confront them and probably would have beat the hell out of them, but Paul stopped him.

"Not worth it," he said. "Save it for the ring."

Jesse swore at them under his breath, and he used some pretty strong adjectives.

Tina swore at them too, not under her breath, and her choice of words was even worse. That was the first time I'd seen Jesse smile.

Then the dressing room door swung shut.

—

Tina was perched on the edge of her seat. She hated being on the outside as an observer; what she really wanted was to be in the corner with her salve and ice packs, shouting commands into Mankiller's ear. Still, a fight's a fight, and even if she couldn't control the outcome, it was the best place my sister could be.

"Pop?" I asked, offering to get refreshments for us.

She grunted something. I think it was "no thanks," but her eyes never left the door from which the fighters were about to emerge.

"Imagine us in ringside seats," I said.

Still no comment.

I looked around. There wasn't a huge crowd, but more than what I thought there'd be for a newcomer like Jesse Mankiller. Pitts was the one they were there to watch, though. He was the one they'd be rooting for.

Suddenly there was a burst of applause, and everyone started shouting and cheering.

"Here we go," said Tina, as wide-eyed as a kid just about to take a ride on a roller coaster.

Mason Pitts, his trainer and cut man came barrelling down the aisle, and there was no mistaking who was the crowd favourite, since every time he lifted his glove in the air, the cheering nearly destroyed my ear drums for life. Tina said something to me, but I couldn't hear her.

Pitts wore a long black robe with his name on the back, and his corner men also had his name on their shirts. Tina kept pointing to them; I think she was mad about Pitts's big budget.

We tried to cheer when Paul and Jesse came out, but it was like trying to light a match in a windstorm; we were squelched by the loud booing that filled the forum. A cut man followed them to the ring, carrying ice packs and bandages and gauze pads.

Jesse didn't give a damn about the jeers. He looked great in his white robe that had "Mankiller" written across the back in bright red, like his gloves. Very simple. Very sharp. Tina nodded her approval. I approved, too, but I think it might have been his long ponytail and washboard abdomen that steered my vote.

He slipped gracefully between the ropes, sat down on his stool and listened as Paul whispered instructions into his ear. Pitts looked foolish, jumping up and down and throwing out punches into space.

The ring announcer spoke into a microphone. "Ladies and gentlemen," he started. When the noise level remained several decibels above deafening, he tried again, this time harder. "Ladies and gentlemen," he shouted, "a ten round bout."

Tina's eyes caught Jesse's as he stood up, and she started screaming advice at him. He ignored her, choosing instead to flirt with a young woman who stuck her hand through the ropes and slipped him her phone number. Paul got rid of her quickly.

The announcer continued, making sweeping motions with his free hand. "In this corner, wearing black trunks and weighing in at one hundred seventy-three pounds, from Halifax, Nova Scotia ... MASON PITTS." The crowd went crazy.

"And in this corner, in white trunks" – the booing was loud and steady, with a smidgen of polite applause from older members of the audience and whistles from every woman with seeing eyes – "weighing one hundred seventy-two pounds, originally from Oklahoma, now living in Truro, Nova Scotia ... Jesse Mankiller."

Tina and I cheered and cheered, but it felt like being in one of those dreams where you want to run from something, but your feet won't move.

The referee signalled the two fighters into the centre of the ring and repeated the rules and instructions; neither one heard a word of it. Then they tapped gloves, went back to their corners and waited for the bell.

By the time it sounded, Tina was standing on top of her chair and several men behind her were hollering at her to get out of the way. She didn't. Soon they were squeezed between our chairs, breathing down my neck.

Jesse strolled out at the bell and was more relaxed than any fighter I'd ever seen. He was in no rush, and let Pitts throw the first punch. He ducked it deftly, like he was equipped with the radar of a bat, and when Pitts was wide open, Jesse sent him a left hook to welcome him aboard. That smartened up the Halifax fighter, and from that point, his arm started pumping. Jesse let him do it.

"That's right!" hollered Tina. "Wear him out, Mankill-er. Give him the rope. He'll hang himself!"

Nobody sits higher on the stump than my sister when it comes to knowing how to win a boxing match, but even I could see that Jesse was the better fighter.

"He's good, isn't he?"

"He's good," said Tina. And she expected a lot from a boxer. So if she said he was good, it meant he could win a title. "He'll take it by the fourth round," she added.

I thought so too.

But after the first round, Jesse hollered something to Paul about his opponent being greased – an illegal act in boxing, where the cut man has applied Vaseline to an area other than the forehead.

Tina got wind of it and started screaming at Pitts's manager and the referee, but nobody took notice. That was until she headed over to their side, threw both hands in the air and told them to keep their (she swore here) finger out of the (another one) Vaseline jar.

When the bell rang, Pitts came out with a long, loopy right that Jesse moved around effortlessly. Then they met in the middle, and for one crazy minute it was nothing but a sea of jabs and hooks until Jesse danced out, leaving Pitts twisting in pain.

He came at Jesse again, and this time Pitts connected. There was a stream of blood running down Jesse's face and it was interfering with his sight.

Paul and the cut man tried to stop the blood from gushing, but the best they could do was slow it down to a lighter but steady flow.

"See." Tina's eyes flashed with anger. "Paul has no time to instruct Mankiller if he's too busy cleaning him up. Nobody can handle that, Ellie."

She was right. Paul looked tired already. Sick, even.

Tina took over from the sidelines.

"Take him out, Mankiller," she hollered. "Jab with the right to push him back," she told him. "Then cross to the head."

He couldn't hear her.

The bell rang and in no time he had Pitts against the ropes. He moved in close for a short hook.

Two good punches and the fight was his. Or at least it would have been.

Just as Jesse was going in for what would have been the knockout punch, there was a blood-curdling scream from the crowd. Then another. Then dozens more.

Paul Holley had collapsed.

CHAPTER NINE

When I woke up, I was slumped in a chair in a waiting room on the main floor of the Halifax Infirmary. It took several minutes for me to get my bearings, then I remembered.

"Is Paul – is he going to live?" I asked Bonita.

She and Tina and I had spent all night waiting for news. Louise Holley was next door, in a special area close to the intensive care unit, for relatives only.

"I don't know, Ellie." Bonita had chewed her nails right down to the quick.

Tina said nothing. She kept closing her eyes and squeezing her knees together; I could tell she was in pain from having sat there too long. Every once in a while she gazed up at the sterile blue and white walls, and I figured she was imagining her own future, having to spend the better part of a year in a similar prison.

"How long was I asleep?"

"Not long," answered Bonita, but it must have been hours because I saw daylight streaming in through the windows.

"Where's Jesse?" I asked.

"He had to go home," said Tina. "Tend to his mother."
I looked at Bonita. She was exhausted.

"If you'd like to go home and take a nap, I can call you if there's any developments," I offered. But as it turned out, my suggestion wasn't necessary because Louise came through the door.

"Louise!" Bonita jumped up.

"He's going to be okay – eventually." Paul's wife threw herself into the nearest chair and let her head fall back. The three of us let out sighs of relief.

"Oh, thank God," said Bonita, grabbing her friend's arm.

Louise put a hand on Tina's shoulder.

"The cardiologist told me that your decision to cover him with ice packs may have saved him from suffering brain damage. It may even have saved his life." She leaned over and hugged my sister with the bit of strength she had left.

Tina shrugged it off, but I knew she was pleased with herself. When Paul collapsed, she had raced up onto the ring and grabbed the ice from both corners; somehow she knew that cooling his body could protect his brain, while the ringside physician revived him and got blood flowing again.

"It's not a well-known technique," mumbled Tina. "I read about it somewhere."

Ring magazine, no doubt.

"What did you mean – he'll be okay 'eventually'?" Bonita asked Louise.

"Paul is going to have to stay here for at least two weeks. Maybe longer. They'll have to monitor his heart until they get his medication right." She drew a long breath. "He can deal with that, I know he can. But he won't be managing any boxers. Never again."

"Too much stress?" I guessed.

"Way too much," answered Louise. "I'm not saying he can't watch from the sidelines, but he can't be responsible for anybody's career, that's for sure." She sighed heavily. "I don't know how he's going to deal with it."

"What about Jesse?" asked Tina.

Louise shook her head slowly back and forth. "I don't know how to tell him."

"He was robbed last night," said Tina. "They should have awarded him a technical decision based on points. Any fool could see he was going to win."

"Why didn't they?" asked Bonita.

"Rules say you can't have a winner based on points unless it goes four rounds." Tina pounded her fist against her knee. "Mankiller had that fight."

"Who's going to tell him that Paul can't manage him anymore?" I asked.

No one had an answer. Then Tina spoke up.

"I am," she said.

—

When Jesse appeared at the hospital the next day, Tina gave him the bad news.

He let it glance off him like an uppercut to the jaw.

"Okay," he said, walking away like she'd casually mentioned that it looked like rain.

Tina followed him to the vending machine. He kicked it and a can of orange soda flew out.

"I can do it," she said.

"You can do what?" He pulled open the can and it fizzed out the top. He threw his lips over it and I felt those weird butterflies in my stomach again.

"I can be your manager."

He laughed.

"I can. Paul's set up the Amherst fight with the promoter and the one in Portland after that. Win those and you're on your way to Boston."

"Give me a break, will you?" He tossed back more soda. "Look, you're a nice girl and everything and I'm sure you know a lot about boxing, but I really don't want a manager right now. I can handle it myself."

"You're going to fight without a manager?"

"I don't know. I haven't made up my mind."

Louise Holley came out of Paul's room and said that he insisted on seeing us but that we could only talk to him for a minute. Tina, Jesse and I went in; Bonita stayed with Louise outside the room.

"Hey, man," said Jesse, grabbing Paul's hand with both of his and leaning over him for a hug. He couldn't get past all the tubes and cords, but the feeling was definitely there.

"I'm sorry, Jesse." Paul struggled with the words. "You had that … fight."

"Forget it, okay? Just get better. That's what I want, you hear me?"

"And you," said Paul, pointing at Tina. "I owe you so much."

Tina blushed. I think I blushed too.

"Why?" asked Jesse, and when I explained what the cardiologist had said, the boxer raised his eyebrows and, in his own aloof way, was somewhat impressed.

"Will you take over for me, Tina?" Paul asked, his speech slurred. "Can you do that for me?" He took a few shallow breaths. "Everything is set up – the motel rooms, the contracts, everything."

Tina was stumped. She didn't want to upset Paul by admitting that she'd already asked and Jesse didn't want her help. And she couldn't agree to his request knowing that Jesse didn't want her.

"Look, Paul," said Jesse. "There's no saying that I'm going to be asked to fight in Amherst."

"They'll want you, Jesse." Paul fought to get out the words. "That bout was yours. The promoter knows that you're the draw now." He looked at Tina again. "You'll get him there?"

"I'll do whatever I can," she said, giving Jesse a look that, if it was audible, would have been something akin to "if this stupid ass of a boxer will get off his throne and stop acting like the world owed him something."

A nurse made us leave the room, and I think it was a good thing she did because neither Tina nor Jesse wanted to lie to Paul.

Outside the room, Jesse took Tina aside and gave her the brush off.

"Thanks, but no thanks. I'm not even sure I'm going to be boxing anymore, okay?"

"You'd be a damn fool to let talent like yours go to waste," declared my sister. "I've trained a lot of boxers—"

"Oh, come on," said Mankiller.

"She has," I argued. "Our father has a gym in Sydney and Tina's been working with the paperweights, and— "

"Featherweights, Ellie."

"Right."

"As I was saying," Tina continued valiantly, "I've worked with many boxers and I know exactly what it takes to get you to the top. You've got it. You've got what it takes, and you'd be stupid not to use it."

"I don't care anymore," said Jesse. He took his pop can, crushed it in his hand and tossed it into a garbage can ten feet away. "Too many strikes against me, okay? Too many problems to deal with right now."

"You mean your mother? And Meryl?" I asked.

There was fire in Jesse's eyes when he replied.

"My mother needs more care than I can give her. My sister is an alcoholic. I think she's trying to kill herself with it and honestly, some days I don't blame her. Okay?" He turned his back on us and walked away.

Tina shook her head and wheeled around to face me.

"And now you know why he's such a fantastic boxer."

CHAPTER TEN

I truly enjoyed spending a couple of weeks at Bonita's place, although I wished it had been under better circumstances. As the days progressed and it became clear that Paul was going to require further rehabilitation, I realized that we'd soon have to leave her little cottage on the tree-lined street. It depressed me to think about heading back to the Pier and back to the grubby old gym.

As I expected, Bonita sat us down and told us she wasn't going to make the trip to New England; Louise needed her now more than ever. She needed someone to look after her children while she drove back and forth to Halifax, and she needed someone to be there for moral support.

I told Bonita not to worry about us, that we understood perfectly and that we'd take the train home to Sydney.

Tina told Bonita not to worry about us, that we understood perfectly and that she'd be taking the train to Boston.

"You can't do that," argued Bonita. "I'm responsible for you two."

"I'm eighteen," declared Tina decisively, like she was joining the army or trying to get into a restricted movie. "And I can look after Ellie."

"I can look after myself." I lifted my chin. "*If* I decide to go with you."

"You can come with me or not," declared Tina. "Choice is yours." She headed into the guest room to start packing her things.

"I'm sorry," said Bonita. "I feel terrible because I promised you guys. But I can't leave Louise, not now."

"I know," I said.

"You don't have a driver's licence, do you?"

"No, I don't."

"And Tina can't drive, of course," said Bonita, prompting Tina to yell her response from the other room.

"She would if she could reach the pedals."

Bonita wrinkled up her forehead as if to say, "I wish she hadn't heard that."

"I saw that," teased Tina.

Bonita laughed.

"Why did you ask if I had a driver's licence?" I asked.

"You could have taken Tina to Boston in Brandy. I don't need the car, because I'll be staying with Louise."

"I wish I had my licence," I replied, "but I can't afford a car anyway."

"No, I guess you can't." Bonita went into the kitchen to make us some lunch. She started cutting up a tomato, then suddenly threw down the knife.

"I've got an idea!" she said.

Tina appeared at the door to hear what it was.

"Jesse Mankiller. He has a licence. No car, but I do believe he drives, because Paul said he was looking for work and figured a licence would help him find a job."

She smiled. "He could take you girls to Boston in my car. I'd feel better if you weren't on your own."

"He won't take me to Boston," mumbled Tina. "And I refuse to tell him about my operation anyway."

"You don't have to, Tina," said Bonita. "Just convince him to fight those fights, make sure he wins and the three of you will wind up in Boston anyway."

Tina gave a little sneer. "You make it sound so easy."

"You said yourself that you could manage him. And he has what it takes to win. Why not give it a try? What have you got to lose?"

—

Bonita drove us over to the reservation that afternoon. Jesse came out of his family's trailer when he saw us pull in, but the greeting we received was icy at best.

"My mother's not good today," he said, which meant we weren't being invited inside. His face was strained and his hair disheveled. "How's Paul?" he asked Bonita.

"About the same. It's going to be a while before he can come home." She leaned against the car. "I'm sorry that he can't manage you anymore, Jesse. I understand you have an excellent career ahead of you."

"No, I don't think so."

Tina listened to him argue with Bonita and took in every nuance of their conversation. Bonita told him how great he was, and how much respect Paul had for his ability in the ring; he argued that fate was against him and that he had too many responsibilities anyway.

I waited and waited for Tina to jump in. I trusted that her response would be the perfect one. And it was.

"Hasn't it ever occured to you, Mankiller, that if you took home the purse in Amherst and Portland and then again in Boston, that you could get a better place for you mother? With a proper ramp?" She lectured him through gritted teeth. "And hasn't it occured to you that showing a bit of strength might be the very thing that your sister needs right now?"

Jesse said nothing. He shrugged her off.

Bonita didn't accept that. "Tina is an excellent trainer," she insisted. "She's been coaching Flyin' Ryan at her daddy's gym."

"Ryan Byrne?"

"Yes. He's looking for some titles himself, and when he wins them, Tina and her father are going to be in demand." She put an arm around my sister, but I don't think she appreciated it much. "Tina's daddy was a world-class boxer, before the … before hurting his hand."

"His hand?" Jesse forced himself to be polite to Bonita, but boredom seeped from every word.

"Forget about it," snapped Tina.

"Okay, I will," said Jesse. His eye caught Tina's. "What the hell do you care about my boxing career anyway? What's it to you?"

"Nothing. But I need to get to Boston and Bonita is offering us her car."

"Why do you have to get to Boston?"

"None of your business."

"Take a bus, why don't you?"

"Just might do that," said Tina.

Jesse said goodbye to Bonita, then went back inside the trailer.

By then, a group of five or six boys had gathered around and, overhearing our conversation, had started up a mock boxing match behind us. The two oldest boys – they looked to be about eight or nine – were pretending to be Jesse and his opponent. The other kids were cheering and shouting.

"Pow, pow," hollered the one who was supposed to be Jesse.

"Mankiller, Mankiller," chanted the boys.

"Knock him out, Jesse!"

"He's down!"

They stood over top of the one who'd "lost" and gave him the count. But they only counted to three and did it way too fast.

"No, no, no," shouted Tina. "That's not the way it works."

My sister couldn't resist any match, even if it was just a child's game.

"Grab that rope over there," she said, pointing to a length of thick yellow string that was hanging from the end of a rusty old canoe, sitting upright against the trailer next to Jesse's.

The kids dashed over and had it back in ten seconds.

"Grab that end," hollered Tina. They pulled the rope around Brandy and a small fence that ran parallel to the car about six feet away. "Good," she declared. "Now, there's your ring."

"Are you a dwarf?" asked one of the boys.

"Yes. For that, you have to be the guy who gets knocked out." She shoved him under the rope.

The plywood door to Jesse's trailer opened, and his sisters ran out to watch. A few more kids appeared out of nowhere. Now there was a regular gang. Bonita pulled a couple of lawn chairs out of her trunk, and she and I sat down to watch the event.

"Okay," said Tina, examining the boys, then pointing to the oldest. "You're going to be the winner."

"I'm Jesse?"

"Yeah, you'll be Jesse. What's your name?"

"Tyler."

"Now, Tyler, you and your friend here are going to do everything I say and there'll be no real punches thrown, just the fake kind, okay? Otherwise you'll have me to deal with."

"Got it," they said in unison.

She told them how the rules of the sport work and how you have to give a guy the ten count – not three – and how to do it properly. Then she drew a line with her foot in the dirt.

"I want both of you toe to the scratch."

"What's that?"

"That's an old boxing term that means both of you are to stand in the centre of the ring until the referee – that's me – tells you to start." She sounded an imaginary bell then moved aside.

They went at it, and she stopped them again.

"No! You're all wrong." She ducked under the rope. "Keep your chins down, that's the only way to keep from getting your block knocked off." She pushed the boys' heads down. "Now use your strong arm – right if you're right-handed – use that for defense. Use it to block the oncoming punches. Your left fist is for punching." She bounced around and showed them how to duck and bob. "And always think in combinations: left jab, straight right, left hook." She demonstrated that, too. "And every once in awhile, give them something they don't expect, like a bolo punch."

The boys started to laugh.

"What's a bolo punch?" asked Tyler.

"That's a flashy uppercut that is more about showing off than it is about power. Just to let your opponent know who's boss."

The kids went back to their boxing match and already you could see a difference in the way they were sparring. Bonita and I started chanting, just like it was a real match, and the kids in the audience joined in too.

"Okay, boys," said Tina, standing between them as a miniature referee. "Now I want you to learn the candy cane."

"The what?" asked Tyler.

"The candy cane."

"What's that?" asked his opponent.

Tina was about to answer when Jesse stepped over the rope, strolled inside the ring and answered for her.

"That's a body punch used by Sugar Ray Robinson. It's thrown with the right hand, slightly turned over and driven downward. Isn't that right, Miss MacKenzie?"

"It's your turn to show the kids some moves, Mr. Mankiller," she said, joining Bonita and me at the side-lines. The boys enjoyed sparring with their hero, and I enjoyed watching him. Jesse seemed happy in that setting, in an old pair of sweats that were ripped at the knee, his body relaxed and comfortable.

He's absolutely gorgeous, I said to myself.

And when I looked at Tina, I could tell that buried somewhere beneath the remnants of a lifetime of pugilism, there was a young woman. And she thought he was gorgeous too.

The afternoon wound down, and the kids went home for dinner, so we folded up the rope and Bonita put the chairs back into the trunk. I thought Jesse would head straight home too, but instead he opened up the car doors for us.

"Tina?" he mumbled.

"Yeah?"

"Thanks for spending time with the boys like that. Thanks for not dismissing them."

"I never dismiss anyone," she said.

"Because …?"

"Because I've been dismissed my entire life and I don't like it very much."

Jesse thought for a minute. "I wasn't dismissing you."

"Look, I don't care, Mankiller. If you don't want to fight, you don't want to fight."

Jesse glanced at the trailer, and I knew he was thinking about the money he could win.

"See you around," said Tina, slamming the car door.

He opened the back door next to me. Then he ducked down to talk to Bonita. I felt his hair brush against the top of my arm.

"If the offer's still on, I'd appreciate the loan of your car."

CHAPTER ELEVEN

"Now you girls will be careful, won't you? You know Mama. She would never let me forget it if anything happened to you. As it is, I don't know how I'll ever get up the nerve to tell her that I sent you off in my car with a stranger." She poured us each a cup of tea. "I think Jesse's a good guy. I really do. I know that Paul and Louise think a lot of him, and there's no way they'd let you two travel with him if he was a bad guy."

Bonita had risen early the next morning to prepare a lovely breakfast of fresh fruit and pastries, the polar opposite of the stuff we had at home. If I didn't have time to prepare something nice, Tina and my father would satisfy themselves with bargain brand cereal eaten out of a chipped bowl.

"You don't have to tell Azalea anything," Tina said. "By the time you and Ellie are back at the Pier, I'll be settled in Boston and you can explain everything to her then."

Every time she said the word Boston, the worst scenarios streamed like a movie through my mind; most of them involving my sister being chopped into pieces. I tried to think happy thoughts instead. I thought about Tina and Jesse and me and all the fun we were going to have. The freedom of it all!

"Paul is delighted that you are going to be there to coach Jesse. He says everything is set up for Jesse's lodgings, but what about you two?"

"We'll be fine, Bonita," declared Tina. "There'll be no problems. And don't worry about Mankiller being girl-crazy – I'll watch out for Ellie."

Yeah, thanks, Tina. Be sure to keep him away from me. I'd hate to have him try anything.

"Who'll watch out for you?" asked Bonita.

Tina smirked. "Oh come on," she said. "I don't have to worry about men being interested in me."

"Don't be so sure," insisted Bonita, but we all knew she was just trying to be nice. She didn't press the point and inquired instead about Jesse's mother. "Who's going to look after her and the girls while he's gone?"

"I asked him that when he called last night," said Tina. "His aunt – I guess she's his mother's sister – has agreed to stay with her for as long as necessary."

"Good," said Bonita, "then everything's set."

"I need to pick up a few things at the pharmacy, and then we're good to go," said Tina.

"You've got enough of that styptic salve to last a year," I said.

"Right, but you're going to need some Adrenaline hydrochloride and Avitene."

"What do you mean *I'm* going to need some Adrenaline hydrochloride and Avitene?"

"Oh, didn't I tell you?" remarked Tina, in her anyone-can-do-anything voice. "You're going to be our cut man."

—

The drive to Amherst was probably the best hour of life on earth I'd ever spent. Tina insisted on riding in the back seat, and when I asked her about seeing nothing but the back of my head, she made a face and mouthed "shut up" when Jesse wasn't looking. I think she felt stupid riding next to him. Or maybe just short. I don't know, but I loved it.

I saw people staring at us when we slowed down for stoplights, and I knew why. Jesse looked like a movie star, his long black hair blowing behind him. And that car! Brandy has to be the coolest automobile in Nova Scotia, and to be riding next to Jesse Mankiller with the top down – well, it was the closest to heaven I'd ever been. Even if it did mean being a cut man. I'd have agreed to clean out the spit buckets if it meant I could ride in Brandy with Jesse.

Tina said nothing all the way there. I wanted her to enjoy the experience, but she kept any trace of joy to herself, so not a shred of human being showed. She wrote things down into a little pad, and it all looked very important. She wanted us to think she was working on a strategy for the fight, but when I sneaked a peek, it was nothing but doodles. Hundreds of doodles.

Our first stop in Amherst was the motel, and that's when my stingy, penny-pinching sister decided to inform me that we'd be sharing Jesse's room.

"You will?" asked Jesse, with a seductive smile. I knew he was only joking, but once again my stomach did a back flip. Then he changed his tune. "Look, you girls had better get your own room. I don't want to be accused of anything. I've got damn near every father in Truro after me already."

"Forget it, Mankiller," said Tina. "And stop thinking with your— you know. If you took thirty seconds to think with your brain instead of your boxing shorts, you'd realize that Ellie and I will be a hell of a lot safer sharing a room with you than we would be on our own. You're a prizefighter, for God's sake. Start acting like a prizefighter, and stop thinking like a gigolo."

That shut him up.

We didn't waste any time checking in; the fight was scheduled for that evening, and Tina wanted to get a feel for the location, the ring and the promoter. We did take time to eat a proper meal, though, for Jesse's sake, and after that, headed to the arena.

Tina barked orders as we marched through the hall looking for the dressing room.

"Enswell? Where's the enswell?" she asked me, referring to the metal thing that's kept on ice, then used to put pressure on cuts.

"Look, Tina," I said sulkily, "I don't know anything about being a cut man."

"You'll do fine," she said.

And although it was reassuring to know she trusted that I'd do the right thing, I had a sneaking suspicion that when put to the test, I'd probably be better at cleaning the spit buckets.

Tina pushed open the dressing room door and found it full of naked and semi-naked men. All the fighters on tap for that night had to share one room, and they let out a big roar when we came in.

The promoter introduced himself, then escorted us out.

"I'm Mankiller's manager," declared Tina.

The promoter couldn't stop himself from laughing; I don't know if it was because Tina was a young woman, or a dwarf, or both. Either way, he found the whole thing funny.

Tina did not.

"We'll need our own room," she insisted.

"Forget about it," he said.

"Then we won't fight."

Jesse looked puzzled.

"Which will be too bad for you," my sister continued, "because after what happened to my boxer in Halifax, the crowd is waiting to see what he can do." She put down her bags and folded her arms in front. "Mankiller had that fight. Every sports writer in the province has made that clear. And that's the only reason you've managed to put so many backsides into seats in this crummy place tonight."

The promoter said nothing at first, then he took us to our dressing room. It was a lot nicer than the first one.

Tina spoke to him about some of the details of the event, what Jesse's share of the gate receipts would be, and then asked to see the ringside physician. They went into a little room someplace, where she had to reveal the contents of her miracle salve – those were the rules. She didn't have to give the exact proportions – those will go to the grave with her – but she did have to disclose the ingredients.

While I unloaded our supplies, Jesse went for his weigh-in and returned ready to fight.

Tina wound gauze over Jesse's knuckles and gave him the dope on who he had to face in the ring.

"You're fighting Thunder Donnelly," she said matter-of-factly. "I've seen him in Sydney. He's an outside fighter, keeps a big gap and moves fast with long-range punches."

"Donnelly's good," admitted Jesse.

"You're better," insisted Tina. "Keep out of his way, let him throw some pitty-pat punches, then kill him."

She wound tape over the gauze, across his fingers, down his hand and around his wrist. My sister had taped so many hands, she could do it blindfolded.

"Okay, Ellie," she hollered, "start rubbing his thighs."

"What?"

"You heard me. His thighs."

I started to shake and Jesse winked at me playfully, which made me shake even more.

"Oh, for heaven's sake. Don't be such an idiot." She got down on her hands and knees and kneaded the muscles of his thighs to show me how it was done.

"Hey," teased Jesse, in a sexy voice, "this is sweet. Two girls massaging me. Keep it up and I won't be fighting anytime soon."

"Shut up," growled Tina.

She forced me to rub his legs, but I stayed much further south than she did; his knees were the best warmed up knees in the history of boxing.

"Let's go," said Tina, putting training mitts on each hand and prompting Jesse to start jabbing. The next ten minutes was an unsettling combination of uppercuts, straight rights and left hooks tossed up with a healthy dose of my sister's screams, hollers and jeers.

She told him he was too slow.

She told him he was too weak.

She told him he wasn't working hard enough.

She told him he was nothing but another bozo on the bus.

Then she tied back his hair, rinsed off his mouth guard, slammed him in the middle of the back and assured him he had the bout nailed.

"Thunder's got a short right uppercut," Tina told Jesse. "Keep him outside, and when he goes for your jaw, hook to his rib cage, then his chest, and when he drops his arm, go for his chin. And whatever you do, Mankiller, take your time. Stick and move, stick and move."

When we headed into the arena, coloured spotlights shot at us from above like we were criminals who'd just scaled the barbed wire, and deafening music blasted from a huge long line of speakers. Unlike at Halifax, there were people cheering for Jesse this time; I could hear them shouting his name.

He looked fantastic as usual in his white trunks and robe, banging his red gloves together and snapping his long ponytail from side to side. Women were whistling and throwing themselves (not to mention their underthings) at him when he passed their seats.

Tina walked bravely behind; it was hard for her to have that many eyes staring at her, but thankfully, Jesse was the main attention-grabber that night, and most of the gapes were headed his way. I followed her, carrying the ice bucket, the enswell, the spit bucket and sponges. Tina had the salve and potions. And the knowledge.

Since everything I knew about boxing could be written on the head of a pin, I felt like I'd joined an exclusive club on forged credentials.

"Okay, Mankiller," announced Tina. "It's time to rock."

CHAPTER TWELVE

The first round was as uneventful as a Sunday in Sydney. Thunder Donnelly threw out an uppercut to Jesse's groin, but he dodged it. Just as Tina told him to do, he let his opponent waste a good deal of energy with long, slow punches.

After the bell, while Tina whispered a bunch of stuff into his ear, I sponged Jesse's neck, tilted up his water bottle and let him spit some out, then rinsed his mouthpiece. Exactly the kind of stuff that made my skin crawl back home, but somehow I didn't mind looking after Jesse. He always smelled good, even when dripping with sweat.

The second round was much like the first, and finally, by the third, Tina told him it was time to go for the jugular.

The two fighters met in the middle of the ring, slugging and going at each other so fast now that I couldn't tell who was getting hit. One of Donnelly's rights connected with the bridge of Jesse's nose. *Crack!*

The blood started spurting in every direction.

The crowd went wild. People were jumping on top of their seats for a better look.

Tina screamed her guts out.

"Jab with the right, jab with the right!"

Jesse hurled Donnelly against the ropes, but the bell rang.

"Damn!" hollered Tina.

She threw the salve at me.

"I can't get it to stop!" I cried, using the cold enswell and then the ice and then the salve.

"Not like that! It's not tanning lotion, for God's sake."

Tina pinched the flesh hard, then fingered her ointment right into it like she was stuffing a deviled egg. And the whole time she was cleaning him up, she was shouting instructions at him.

Now that Jesse'd been cut, it was going to be a tough fourth round. He started out sharp, pushing Donnelly around the ring, but Thunder knew enough to aim for the wound. Then he rammed his head into Jesse's face. And even when the referee was in the process of breaking them up, Donnelly took another stab at the cut. The referee warned him, but he didn't care. He'd do anything to win the match, and Tina knew it.

We cleaned Jesse up again, and the salve was doing its job wonderfully well. Still, the slams that Jesse was taking from Donnelly kept re-opening the wound, and the blood flow was interfering with his vision. It was Halifax all over again.

"You've got the skill, now go for the kill," said Tina. "Let him have the first one, and when he's open, stick him with the best left hook you've ever delivered."

She tossed him back into the ring, and following her instructions to the letter, he let Donnelly throw the first punch, a hard jab that glanced off his chin and left Donnelly wide open for the belt that crushed his cheekbone and sent him flying.

Jesse went at him again, this time with a straight right. Thunder staggered backward, and I figured things were going to end right there, but he came back fiercer than ever. He muscled in on Jesse, dropped his shoulder and threw another uppercut to the groin.

Jesse writhed in pain.

The bell rang.

I sponged him like crazy. And I tried to clean up his cuts. Tina didn't have time.

"This is it, Mankiller," she said. "It's got to be done in this round or we're going to lose you. I've stopped the worst bleeding, but Donnelly's opening it up every chance he gets. And now he's going below the belt." Tina held up the water bottle for him, and Jesse spat it out in one long stream into the bucket. Then he opened his mouth for her to replace the mouthpiece. She kept hollering stuff at him.

"He's stupid, Mankiller, and you're not. I want you to jab with the right – do you hear me, Mankiller?"

He was dazed and couldn't talk, but he nodded.

"Jab with the right, just to push him back, okay? When his shoulder drops for the uppercut – that's his style, Mankiller, that's what's coming next, I know it – when he goes for that uppercut I need you to hook to the head."

The crowd screamed like mad when the boxers came back, rushing together and pumping out punches and banging their heads together.

Jesse was tired, and I could see it.

Donnelly circled to the right of him, biding his time, waiting for the chance to try another one of his cheap shots. And then, just like Tina said he would, he dropped his shoulder and prepared for the uppercut, but Jesse throttled him with a left hook to his noggin.

Thunder Donnelly fell backwards against the ropes.

The crowd went wild. They screamed for the ref to call the fight.

"They want him to call it so Jesse doesn't win," Tina told me, driving her fist into the stool. "If the ref calls it now, they could be tied with points. The judges could even rule for Donnelly." She cupped her hands and shouted through them as though her life depended on it. "Take him out now," Tina screamed, "or they'll hand it to this jerk on a platter."

Jesse heard her. He surged forward like a leopard, then moved on him with a devastating series of short, powerful punches, and Donnelly went down like a colossal stone megalith.

Thunk!

The referee gave him the ten count, but he could have counted to five hundred, it wouldn't have mattered. Thunder wasn't getting up anytime soon.

The crowd roared so loud I couldn't tell if they were for us or against us, but I didn't really care. We'd won, and Jesse Mankiller was going to Portland, Maine, for his biggest fight yet.

The referee grabbed Jesse's right arm and held it high in the air.

In my opinion, Tina should have been out there with him, sucking up some of the glory.

She was covered in blood, sprayed with sweat and smelled like an old root cellar from that salve of hers, but I was proud of my sister. Really proud.

—

"It was a barnburner!" squealed Tina into the phone. "Did you listen to the fight?" Her voice was so deafening, Paul Holley must have thought he'd mistakenly been connected with the ring announcer.

"They wouldn't let me anywhere near a radio," I heard him say. "Where's Jesse now?" Paul's voice was loud too, and Tina held the phone out so I could hear.

"He's lying down," answered my sister. "We're calling from the motel lobby. Sorry it's so late, but you said—"

"I've been waiting for your call! I don't care what time it is!"

"And I'm sorry we had to call collect, but—"

"I told you to! Enough with the sorries, okay? I'm so happy I could jump right out of this hospital bed."

We could hear Louise in the background, giving Paul hell.

"Mankiller took a lot of punishment tonight," said Tina. "He's got to rest up if we're going to win in Maine next week. Most fighters wouldn't attempt three bouts in a row, but he can do it."

"Yeah, but if he wins the North American title in Boston, he can write his own ticket. He can decide when and if he wants to fight. Until then, you'll have to keep him in top shape, Tina. If he takes the U.S. title in Portland, I want to be there in Boston for the big night."

Louise started arguing with him. Then we heard Paul say, "If I *don't* go and watch, I'll be dead. From boredom!"

"How are you doing, anyway?" Tina asked Paul.

"I'm all right. But they've been stickin' so many needles in me, you'd think they were hooking a rug." He chuckled. "I'm going home soon, though."

"That's good," said Tina. "Paul?"

"What is it?"

"Jesse wonders if you could ask Louise to ask Bonita to check in on his Mom and sisters. They don't have a telephone, and he's worried about them. If she could, it would put his mind at ease."

"And I want his mind at ease!" declared Paul. "Tell Jesse not to worry over his family, we'll look after things. And you keep calling me, will you, Tina? I want to be in the loop, do you hear?"

Louise hollered at him again, but he kept on talking.

"Say, did you hear about Flyin' Ryan Byrne, Tina? I read in the paper that he won in Glace Bay. He's the Eastern Canadian champ now. Look, I gotta go, but keep in touch, will you?"

We headed outside and walked around the back of the motel to our room. Even though I didn't like Ryan very much, I was happy for Dad that he had won; when I admitted it to Tina, she grunted something about it being a fluke. Just as the door to our room came into view, a dark blue Jaguar pulled in slowly past us; the driver parked directly behind Brandy, as if he was trying to make sure she couldn't be moved.

Two men eased their way out of the Jag, ambled around Bonita's car and knocked at our room. One of them was ugly enough to cure hiccups, with deep gullies running from the bridge of his nose to the edges of his mouth. The other one was blond and not ugly, but still looked like he'd kill you for twenty bucks.

"Oh my God." I grabbed Tina's arm. "I know those guys. I've seen them in Sydney; they're mobsters. Dad said so."

"There you go with your gangsters again," mumbled Tina, although by the expression on her face I could tell that she didn't think they were there to collect money for a new church roof.

Jesse opened the door.

"Yeah?" he said, leaning against the door jamb.

"Mankiller, we wanna talk to you." The blond sounded like his throat was full of phlegm.

"Beat it. I don't want whatever it is." He tried to shut the door, but the ugly one stuck his foot in it.

"Oh my God, Tina," I gasped. "I'm getting out of here." I went to run, but she grabbed my shirt and yanked me back.

"Like hell you are."

"But—"

"Come on," she said, dragging me back to our room. I decided that my future was short and black.

The two visitors had Jesse pinned against the wall, and he was swearing at them to get the hell out of our room or he'd crack open their heads.

"Shut up, Jesse," snapped Tina. "Do you want to get yourself killed?" She guessed they were armed, and I'm sure she was right; guys like that wouldn't be caught without a revolver any more than their girlfriends would be seen without makeup.

Jesse didn't heed Tina's warning and continued wrangling with the ugly one. "There's no way in hell that I am going to throw a fight for you or anybody else. I don't give a damn how much money you'll pay me, and your threats don't frighten me."

"You're gonna take a dive, Mankiller. If you don't, you'll never fight again. Get my drift?"

Jesse went to belt him, but Tina grabbed his arm.

"Who's your man in Portland?" she asked.

"Who the hell are you?"

The blond answered. "I've seen her someplace. Whitney Pier – that's it."

"Yeah," agreed the ugly one. "MacKenzie's gym."

Did you have to be a dwarf? I thought. *Did you have to be so memorable?*

"We're from France," I said quickly.

"Damn it, Ellie," barked Tina, "do you have to be so stupid?" She took several steps toward the men. "I am Mankiller's manager, and I decide if he's going to take a dive or not."

"Like hell," mumbled Jesse.

"You didn't answer my question," continued Tina. "The promoter hasn't told me who my boxer is supposed to be fighting in Portland. Cough it up!"

"Judd Stone."

"Stone – oh yeah," said Tina. "He's got the American title now."

"That's right, sweetheart, and we don't want anybody walking off with it," said the blond. "If he doesn't get the chance to fight for the North American crown in Boston, we aren't going to be very happy. And our boss isn't going to be very happy. And when we're not happy, we do crazy things."

"Who's your boss?" Tina asked.

They didn't answer her.

"We'll see you in Portland, Mankiller," said the ugly one, and the two of them left, smiling.

Jesse threw himself down on the bed. "I won't take a dive for anyone."

CHAPTER THIRTEEN

The only part of me that got any sleep that night was my arm. Tina and I were squeezed together in one of the twin-sized beds, which meant I couldn't turn over. And I was too hot. Neither one of us had the nerve to wear a nightgown, so we slept in our clothes. The heat was the worst kind – thick and sticky; the motel had no air conditioning, the fan made a whiny metallic grinding sound and the threats made by the two thugs echoed from the dark recesses of my mind.

Tina slept like a log.

For her, the combination of a profound feeling of accomplishment for winning her first fight as a professional manager, and extreme exhaustion, led her straight to dreamland without a single detour. I was glad she could sleep; I didn't want her to start thinking about the Ilizarov procedure, although even it wouldn't have been as bad as what the two mobsters had in mind for us if Jesse didn't let their guy win.

Jesse had no problem sleeping either. Obviously not the shy type, when he came out of the shower (which was down the hall, across from the front desk, and past six other rooms) he wore nothing but a towel, which he promptly threw to one side of the room before retiring for the night. Tina and I were used to naked men, but Jesse didn't know it; I think he was trying to rattle our cages a bit. Mine was rattled, but it would take a lot more than male anatomy to stir Tina's imagination, so his attempt to show off didn't have quite the impact he might have thought it would.

In fact, Tina continued to drill him about his combination punches even after he'd tossed the towel. From the look on his face, I'd have to say that it was the first time in his skirt-chasing life that a girl – my sister – had not been the least bit impressed by his masculinity.

I guess I must have drifted off at one point, because the sound of Tina and Jesse's bickering startled me. It was about three in the morning. He was asking if she had any aspirin, and she was reminding him what it would do to his blood.

"You'll just have to work through the pain. We've got to get that cut healed or Stone will aim for it as soon as he hears the bell."

Jesse swore at her.

"That's just the pain talking," said Tina.

"You're the only pain that's talking."

Then Jesse mumbled something else – I couldn't make it out – then they were quiet for a minute or two. The room was dark, silent except for the fan and the faint sounds from a party going on a few doors down. I was closest to the window; the motel's neon lights flashed red and blue patches of colour across my pillow.

At one point, Jesse spoke softly to Tina.

"Your old man, he's a boxer, right?"

"Was."

"What happened?"

"Wrecked his hand."

"How?"

"I don't know."

Silence again.

"You don't like your old man?" asked Jesse.

Tina didn't reply.

Then she answered with a question. "Where's your father?" she asked him. "Did he take off on you?"

"Yeah," muttered Jesse in a sarcastic tone. "He was drunk every night on Jack Daniels, never held a job in his life, then he ran off with some buddies of his to rob a bank and now he's in jail." He sighed heavily. "Typical Indian. No good bum."

"All right," said Tina, "I'm sorry I bought into the stereotype and assumed the worst. I apologize, okay?"

It took a few minutes for Jesse to cool off.

"He died in a construction accident. Back in Oklahoma. He worked six days a week and he loved his family more than anything in the world."

"Sorry," said Tina. "You moved to Millbrook after that?"

"Yeah," replied Jesse. "Without our father to support us, my mother came back to Nova Scotia to be with her people."

"Do you like it there?"

Jesse laughed scornfully. "I'm not even going to answer that."

—

Tina didn't want Jesse to spend more than a few hours driving each day; that way she would have plenty of time to force the guy to work out. She had a mean streak, my sister, and loved to watch men suffer at her command. So it was two days before we reached the border at St. Stephen, New Brunswick.

Crossing into the United States at Calais, Maine, was a bit like entering high school; everything – the sky, the trees, everything – looked different somehow. And being on the other side of the Canadian border made it okay for me to wave at people in cars as they drove by, sing out loud with the radio or lie down and stick my feet out the window.

"Get your feet back in the car," said Tina, who, after the win in Amherst, was riding in the front seat again.

"What share of the purse do you want?" asked Jesse, fumbling through his back pocket with one hand while driving with the other. He pulled out his wallet and threw it at her. "Take what you want."

"That belongs to Paul, not me," declared Tina. "You can pay for our meals and motel out of it though. That way I can keep what I have for Boston." She pushed the wallet back at him. "And don't be so eager to give up your share of the profits. The promoters are going to grab enough off you as it is. Hang on to as much as you can for your family." She sneered. "Don't be such an idiot."

She reached for the newspaper she'd picked up in Calais and like a kid to the comics, headed straight to the sports page.

"I guess Paul was right. I couldn't believe it." She kept reading.

"Believe what?" I asked.

"Ryan Byrne did win the Eastern Canadian title."

Jesse turned to her. "I said he was good."

Her eyes never left the page.

"Yeah," she mumbled. "Yeah, now I see," she said.

"What do you see?" Jesse and I asked in unison.

"Schulman was robbed. He should have won. Ref called a technical knockout – said they were both in bad shape and couldn't finish the fight."

"But the fact that Ryan won on points will still help Dad, right?"

Jesse looked at me in the rear-view mirror.

"You need Ryan Byrne to win so your dad gets business, is that it?" he asked me.

"Otherwise we fold and the gym is history," I said.

"Well then," said Jesse to Tina, "be glad that Byrne took the title."

Tina shrugged.

"I thought that gym was important to you?" Jesse asked.

"It is." Tina paused. Then she turned to him. "It's my life."

Jesse kept his eyes on the road for a long stretch of highway, then he starting pumping Tina with questions.

"Why are you going to Boston, anyway? And don't tell me it's none of my business, I'm getting sick of that excuse."

"I'm training to become a gypsy fortune teller."

"Very funny," said Jesse. Then he looked into the mirror at me again. "What's the big secret? Will you tell me?"

"Not unless she wants every hair ripped out of her head." Tina changed the subject. "As you know, Mankiller, this fight in Portland is an important one. That's why we're going to have to take some heat from goons like the pair in Amherst. Win in Portland and it's on to Boston for the North American title. Win that and by September, you're going for the world crown."

Jesse didn't say anything. He just kept motoring along and ignoring her like a cab driver would ignore chitchat or a garbage man would flies.

Then it hit him.

"So are you going to be around in September? Will you still be in Boston when I get back there?"

"I ... I, uh ... yeah, I'll still be in Boston, but I won't be able to manage you for the big one." She turned to him. "Don't worry, if you win the next two fights, you'll have your pick of any manager from Florida to Cape Breton. I guarantee that."

"Maybe Paul can do it by then," I suggested, but my idea didn't go over well.

"No, Ellie," said Tina, "he won't be able to do it. The stress is too much. Probably kill him."

"Why can't you do it if you're going to be in Boston?" asked Jesse.

"Thought you didn't want me for your manager."

"Thought you weren't good enough."

God, they loved to argue.

"You two never stop!" I said. "You sound like you're married or something."

That did it. That shut them up. Neither one said a word until we stopped for lunch.

We didn't know how long it would be before another truck stop, so the next place would have to do; unfortunately, the next place was Bill's Comfy Diner. Somewhere between Calais and Bar Harbor, it was the epitome of everything you didn't want in a restaurant.

"Complete Meal – 3.95" advertised the diner in its fly-specked window, while the greasiest, most unappetizing smells oozed out of a big metal thing on the roof. I don't know who Bill was, but I figured if he ate there very often, he was probably pushing up daisies by now.

There was a stained, yellowed menu pasted on the door and a stack of them on a table inside. Tina told Jesse and me to try to find something decent to order while she made a phone call from the desk.

"Who are you calling?" I asked her.

"Don't worry about it."

"Are you calling Dad?"

"No, Ellie," replied Tina with a sneer. "I'm calling the poison control centre in advance, so I know what to do when we all start collapsing after a meal in this place."

She talked to someone for at least five minutes (and it must have been a collect call, because there was no way that Bill would spring for it) then joined us in a grimy booth.

"Hello, good day, what can I do for you folks today?"

The twenty-year-old waitress approached the table with a practised cheerfulness, but when she noticed Tina was a dwarf, the smile dropped off her face. Her way of coping with the awkward situation was to never let her eyes fall anywhere near my sister. She looked at me, she looked at Jesse, but when it came time for Tina to order, she said, "What will you have?" while keeping her gaze firmly fixed on her order pad.

"How do you stand it?" asked Jesse, once the waitress had left for the kitchen. "Do you count your blessings or something?"

"I would if I had any."

"Crap," said Jesse.

"What the hell blessings have I got?" She thought for a minute. "You're no blessing. You're a pain in the—"

"I didn't say I was a blessing." He took a swig of water. "I just wanted to know how you dealt with idiots like her. What do you do? Imagine them falling off a cliff or something?"

"Don't be stupid," snapped Tina. "Lay off, okay?"

Jesse turned to me. "Is your sister always such a crab?"

"In a word, yes."

"Well, then," offered Jesse, turning to Tina, "I guess we know which one of the seven dwarves you are. And it isn't Bashful."

CHAPTER FOURTEEN

We'd driven about fifteen miles past the diner, and must have been at least twenty from the next town when it happened. I heard what sounded like a small explosion in the engine, then Brandy went *thunk thunk thunk* and Jesse turned off the highway and down a country road. He pulled onto the shoulder and wound up at the end of someone's lane. The mailbox read, "Dot and Ellwood Valentine."

Weeds and brush and shrubs and bushes dominated the landscape, but there was a house in there, its roof barely peeping over the greenery.

Brandy needed time to cool off before we could even look at her engine. Jesse checked the trunk for extra coolant. The jug was almost empty.

"Oh, God," said Tina. "What are we going to do now?"

"Don't have too many options." Jesse unfurled the convertible top and locked the car doors. "We'll see if these people have some coolant; if not, we'll have to call for help."

We marched up the long, overgrown lane. The sky was clear and blue overhead, with billowy white clouds floating effortlessly across the sky. On either side of the driveway a row of bored-looking pine trees grew so idly, you'd swear they were yawning as you passed by.

A few buildings became visible once we were halfway up the lane. The square white clapboard house looked like if you blew hard enough, it would come down in pieces. Several barns in various stages of disintegration stood precariously among the weeds, and we had to skirt around so many old cars and parts of old cars that I thought the place must have previously been a junkyard or the terminus of a dead-end road from which some poor souls had never returned. The only other explanation was that the Valentines' farm had been the landing site of the refuse from a passing tornado; broken lawn chairs, bicycles and tricycles and steering wheels and fenders were strewn a half mile in every direction from the house.

The tornado must have hit the house, too, because part of the roof had blown off, and shingles were lodged in the grass, hanging from trees and caught in bramble bushes.

We kept walking, and before long the front porch was visible. Across it sat an entire family: Mom and Dad and what appeared to be about seven or eight kids – you couldn't tell because the younger ones kept chasing each other in and out the front door. The parents and two teen-aged daughters looked comfortable, reclined in an old car seat that served as a dandy couch. From the same era as Brandy, it was long and red, made of vinyl and cloth and had holes along the edge where white stuff was sticking out.

When the family saw us, the whole bunch of them waved. Not one of those quick little "I wonder who that could be coming up our lane" kind of waves, but rather a greeting normally reserved for a friend you've known forever but haven't seen in years.

I waved back, but Tina and Jesse chose instead to simply nod their heads and plod forward. They were more concerned with getting the car fixed and getting to Portland; I was fascinated by the Valentines.

The one who I figured must be Dot was a large woman in a dirty housedress; her legs were thick and looked like they'd been driven into her shoes. She had long, straight hair that hadn't been trimmed in twenty years. And you could see clear divisions: the oldest swatch was bleached yellow; it ran from her waist almost up to her chest. The next was auburn, then came a greyer version of the auburn and the rest of her hair was just grey. In her right hand was a beer and in her left a cigarette and in her lap was a half-eaten bag of sour cream and onion potato chips. Beside her on the car seat was a copy of *True Confessions* magazine.

"How are you?" she bellowed, and the kids charged at us and grabbed at our clothes and started hollering a bunch of stuff like, "Do you wanna see where my sister found mushrooms and threw up?" and "Our cat had eleven kittens and they're orange."

Dot and Ellwood introduced themselves and all the kids, but the only names I could remember were Darlene and Charlene because they were twins and the same age as me. They had long brown hair, glistening teeth, thick white skin and half-closed eyes. Charlene blinked every time she spoke and had a nasty habit of bending her thumb all the way back to her wrist. She screamed, then giggled, when she noticed Tina was a dwarf.

The eldest of the Valentine children was eighteen-year-old Walter. He was busy working underneath a beat-up old truck, so they pointed at his feet. I think he said something like "Howdy" but can't be sure. He waved at us with an adjustable wrench.

Darlene and Charlene, once they'd taken a good long look at Jesse, ran into the house. Dot kept insisting we sit down; she pushed Ellwood off the end of the car seat with one foot. Then she patted it to encourage Jesse to sit beside her.

"Get these folks a beer," she told her husband, so he opened up a blue metal cooler that was inches away from his ankle and started handing them out.

"No thanks," said Tina.

"You're guests here," said Dot, gesturing to Ellwood to open the bottles and placing the open bag of potato chips on Jesse's knee. He handed them to me, got up and stood next to Tina.

"What we really need is a bit of coolant for our rad," said Tina, "if you can spare some."

At that point, the screen door flapped open and out flew Darlene and Charlene, this time in halter tops that were so low cut, I fully expected something to spill out at any moment. I think Jesse did too because his eyes kept swooshing across their chests like a search light over the water. There was enough makeup plastered on their faces to service a small theatre company, and they'd even found the time to rub on some fake tan but not evenly, so the fronts of their arms and legs were a pumpkin colour, while the backs of their limbs remained as white as crocuses in the snow.

Darlene shoved Tina aside, then grabbed Jesse's arm and started caressing his muscles.

"Where'd you get these?" she said.

"The supermarket," quipped Tina. "Look, I'm sorry, but we've got to get to Portland and all we need is some rad coolant, which we'd be happy to pay for...."

By that time Charlene had Jesse's other arm.

"Walter will fix your car," she said. "Tomorrow." She blinked at Jesse. "You can stay with me tonight."

"You leave him alone, now," scolded Dot, like her daughter was mauling one of the new kittens. I noticed Jesse didn't make an attempt to break free of the girls, and Tina saw it too; she rolled her eyes at Jesse so many times I thought they'd drop out of her head.

"Look," Tina asked Dot, "can you help us or not?" She turned to Jesse. "You haven't said a word."

"You're doing enough talking for all of us."

Ellwood was still opening beers, and when Darlene reached for one, Dot slapped her hand.

"You're not old enough. I don't want folks sayin' I've brung you up wrong," she said, but I had a feeling it was one of those "locking the barn door after the horse was out" kind of things.

Realizing it was Walter that she needed, Tina bent down next to the driver's side of the truck and tried to talk to him, but he just kept banging away at something with a mallet. So she reached inside the cab and honked the horn in order to get his attention, but that only served to get the kids screaming more than they were already. Finally, she grabbed both of Walter's legs and pulled, but he was a bulky guy and she couldn't budge him.

"Stays under there for hours." Dot sucked back some beer. "He'll be out come suppertime." She shook her head. "The boy eats like he's gonna be hung."

"Can he stay for supper?" asked Darlene, caressing Jesse and obviously not the least concerned about Tina and me.

"You'll be our guests," beamed Dot. "I've got stew on." The smell that wafted out of the screen door was about as appetizing as the stuff at Bill's, so I was hoping we could convince Walter to look at the car before having to face dinner with the Valentines.

Tina couldn't stand Darlene and Charlene anymore and out of desperation, drank the beer. Then she wished she hadn't.

When she asked to use the washroom, and they pointed to an outhouse – doorless and sitting a mere ten feet from the porch – I was glad I hadn't accepted anything to drink.

Jesse laughed out loud.

"Go to hell," replied my sister, choosing to walk a half mile through a thicket of bramble bushes and thorns rather than use the facilities.

The Valentines did have indoor plumbing in their house, but the well was nearly dry at that point in the summer and couldn't be used for frivolities like a toilet.

By the time Tina returned, Walter was out from under the car and heading down the lane with Jesse to look at Brandy. The twins still hadn't let go. Ellwood was using the outhouse. And I'd had the pleasure of hearing the de-tails – from conception to birth – of all Dot's pregnancies and miscarriages, along with the four reasons she can't eat lettuce and a list of foods that bind her up.

I changed the subject by asking if they'd always lived there, where the children went to school and if Ellwood was a farmer, but Dot just laughed and didn't answer.

I was relieved to see Tina come out of the woods, al-though she didn't look any too pleased, since the kids had followed her to watch.

"Sit down." Dot patted the car seat again. "Tell me about yourself." When Tina sat down next to her, Dot shoved herself around so she could face my sister. Then nonchalantly, like she was asking her the time or whether she preferred onions in her stew, she looked Tina in the eye and said, "How long will you be in California?"

"Now, Mother," said Ellwood from the outhouse, "that's none of our business."

"California?" Tina didn't know what she was talking about, but I did.

"She thinks you're going to Hollywood," I explained. "You know – to be an actress." It didn't occur to Tina – at least, not right away – that Dot figured all dwarves wind up in Tinseltown.

"What movie are you going to be in?" Dot's eyes were big and round.

Tina's were small and angry. "Look, Mrs. Valentine—"

"Dot." She grabbed my sister's arm. "I know, it's all hush hush with those Hollywood producers."

"Leave the girl alone, Mother." Ellwood stood up; his pants were still down and I looked away.

Dot held up a finger then waddled into the house.

"Where the hell is Jesse?" Tina hissed. "I want out of this place."

When Jesse and Walter returned, it was with our suitcases and the bad news that we weren't going anyplace. Not until a new rad could be found to match Brandy.

"I'm gonna tow her up now," said Walter. "Can't leave a car like that at the road." He left to start up the tractor and fetch a rope.

"We've got no choice," said Jesse.

"Oh, God," I said under my breath.

"Oh, crap," said Tina, not under her breath.

"Oh, good," said the twins, still attached to Jesse.

Dot returned to the porch with a little pink and red book, about the size of a cheque book only plasticized and with a picture of Marilyn Monroe on the front. She handed it to Tina, along with a pen, then started to dictate.

"To Dot, from your devoted friend…."

"What are you talking about?" snarled Tina.

"Your autograph. I want your autograph."

Tina wrote something in there all right, but I could tell by the way she was crossing her t's that it had nothing to do with devotion.

CHAPTER FIFTEEN

Tina and I shared a hot little room upstairs that had one dirty curtain (the other had lost most of its hooks and kept falling off the rod) and one bed. The kids told us that's where their cat had had kittens, and I didn't doubt it because the spread was coated in fur and had stains that I couldn't identify and didn't want to. Large spiders had built webs across every corner of the ceiling and their big white eggs were about to drop onto my head at any minute.

It was a relief, though, not to have that motel sign flashing across my face, and there was a breeze coming through the window. A country breeze – not like the one created by the fan at the motel that felt like it was coming out the back of a clothes dryer.

But I still had trouble sleeping. And this time, so did Tina. I don't think she really cared about the condition of the place, but the fact that Jesse was sleeping in the barn made her uneasy. It wasn't that she objected to his bedding down in a pile of hay, it was whom he was bedding down with that provoked her.

"Yeah," she said, peering through the window toward the barn and pointing like a schoolteacher at a kid with gum, "there they go. I knew it."

I got up to watch as the twins sneaked across the lawn, wearing nothing but tiny nighties and big smiles.

Tina pulled back the curtain, tore off the one that had no hooks, and jerked open the window.

"Where the hell do you think you're going?" she hollered.

"Get lost," said one of them; I think it was Darlene, since she was the twin with the mouth on her.

"Okay, that does it," fumed Tina, pulling on her sweats and heading out to stop them. Or murder them – I wasn't sure.

I ran behind her, down the stairs and out the back door. She didn't feel the thistles, stones and rubble under her feet, and managed to fly to the barn in seconds. I hobbled there, stopping twice to pull tiny bits of sharp gravel from the ball of my foot.

Tina threw open the barn door and found Jesse, a twin on each side of him, in the early stages of what was clearly going to be a long night of pleasure.

"Get out of here," quipped Charlene, and Darlene added her own "thoughts" on the matter, which involved no thinking and quite a lot of swearing.

Tina marched over and told Jesse to get the hell up or she'd quit as his manager.

"Quit. I don't care."

"This kind of thing is exactly what you don't need right now. You need every bit of energy for the ring, you stupid idiot." She grabbed a pitchfork and spiked it hard into the straw, about one inch from Darlene's backside. "Are these two really worth losing for? Are they worth throwing away your chance?" She did the pitchfork thing again, and this time Darlene jumped up. "I didn't think you were so stupid."

"A man has needs. You wouldn't know about that." He pulled Darlene back down beside him.

"What about your family's needs? If you're not in top shape, Mankiller, you will not win the title fight. No way. And frankly, these two …." She stopped herself (I wished she hadn't). "These two are not worth it."

"You wouldn't know if it was worth it or not," he said, and Tina stormed out.

"That was a low blow, Jesse," I said. "My sister didn't deserve that." I left, too.

Tina was in bed by the time I made it back, after stopping again to remove a shard of glass. She didn't acknowledge me, which meant she didn't want to talk.

But I'd discovered a reserve of bravery hidden inside myself, probably nurtured by having to pee in the dark woods (with wild animals, bugs and Walter looming), having to eat Dot's stew (she laughed when I asked what was in it) and having to drink water from a well that was only a stone's throw from the outhouse.

So I asked her, "Tina, are you jealous?"

And had we been in a cartoon (instead of just feeling like we were), that would be the moment when the rest of the Valentines' roof blew off.

—

When we came down for breakfast, Walter was already taking Brandy apart. He enjoyed the process so much, stripping off each piece of the engine with a merciless grin, that I figured Dot must have missed an important detail when she told me about how she conceived Walter – that she'd been dating Dr. Ilizarov at the time.

"Good morning," hollered Ellwood, pouring huge piles of corn flakes into green plastic bowls for us. "Hope the owls didn't keep you up." The kids had already finished eating and were running around outside. Being a staunch believer in the old adage "waste not, want not," Ellwood was busy scraping the leftovers out of their bowls and into his. Darlene and Charlene were sitting side by side and were sure to give us a long and drawn out evil eye when we entered the room.

"The owls didn't," answered Tina, casting a warlike glance at the twins, "but your daughters—"

"Oh, put a sock in it," said Darlene, pushing flakes of cereal under the milk like she was trying to drown them. I could tell by the look on her face, and Charlene's too, that they didn't get too far with Jesse. If they'd been successful, I was pretty sure they'd be quick to gloat about it.

"Where's Dot?" I asked Ellwood.

"Oh, Mother likes to sleep in. You won't see her before noon unless it's Christmas. And it's Johnny's fault."

"Johnny?" I asked, wondering if he was the hired hand and what he was hired for.

"Johnny Carson. *The Tonight Show*." He picked up the empty bowls and dumped them into the sink. "I can't stand the man," he added.

"What's wrong with Johnny Carson?"

"Nothing. But he comes on the same time as my re-runs of *Gunsmoke* and Mother won't let me watch." He got a far-away look in his eyes. "*Gunsmoke*. Now there's a good show." Then he headed to the chicken coop to fetch eggs.

"Where does your father work?" I asked Charlene in an attempt to make conversation.

She ignored me and did that thing where she bent her thumb back.

I tried again. "I'd like to be a teacher. Do you have any profession in mind?"

She didn't reply so Tina answered for her.

"Sure she does. A very old one."

Charlene didn't get it. She shoved her bowl into the middle of the table and went upstairs to get dressed. Darlene followed suit.

"I want the hell out of this place," said Tina.

"We should pay them for the food," I said.

"Whatever."

Jesse came in the side door; he had on faded jeans and a black T-shirt, a string of beads with a feather around his neck, and his hair was braided at the back. When he sat down at the table, my heart did that racing thing again, and I thought to myself that many more days looking at Jesse and his perfect body was going to kill me in the end. I pulled my eyes back into my head as he reached for the corn flakes. Then Walter came in and sent me tumbling back to earth like a parachutist who forgot to pull the cord.

"Yeah," mumbled Walter, rubbing his greasy hands across the front of his round belly. "She needs a new rad all right, and the front fan's in bad shape too. Could do without the fan for awhile, but you're gonna need—"

"Okay, okay," said Tina. "So where do we get one? Can you help us? We'll pay you for your time."

"Oh, that's all right," said Walter, opening up the fridge and taking out a chicken leg. "It's a pleasure to work on a car like that."

"We have to get to Portland in a matter of days," said Tina. "Can you find us a rad, like today?"

"Well now," said Walter, sitting down next to Jesse and taking what seemed to be five minutes to chew and swallow one bite of chicken, "I'm gonna make some calls."

Jesse offered again to pay him for his work. I watched as the twins walked by the kitchen window and crept in the back door. Darlene came up behind Jesse, put her hands over his eyes and said, "Boo!"

Then Charlene did the same, only she said, "Guess who?"

Tina answered for him. "Can't be sure, but there's two of them, and I think they're sharing one brain."

Jesse fought back a smile.

"We're going to pick berries in the back field," said Darlene. "Wanna come?" She gave a super seductive smile, lifted up his braid and rolled it across her chest.

Jesse declined, the girls left (but gave detailed instructions as to where they could be found, should he change his mind and want to indulge in some berry picking and other sweet delights) and Tina wrote a bunch of stuff down in her memo pad. About what, I had no idea, but it made her look important.

I picked up the rest of the bowls, found some detergent under the sink and started washing the dishes. Walter gave me his chicken bones, rubbed his hands on his shirt again, and told us he was going next door to use their phone and try to find us a rad.

"You don't have a phone?" asked Tina, her eyes one step away from a hyena's.

"Did have," said Walter. "Wasn't any use. Dar and Char were on it from sun up to sun down and one night – around ten or so it was – my mother pulled it out of the wall and threw it into the pond." He pointed to where the pond was. I wished they had mentioned the pond sooner, because I'd almost fallen into it during the night, searching for a place to go other than the doorless outhouse.

I kept hoping Jesse and Tina would talk to each other. But they didn't say a word. Tina kept scribbling stuff down, and Jesse looked out the window, clearly preoccupied with something.

Then Tina stood up, pushed back her chair and announced that she had worked out seven new combinations for Jesse, and he was to change into his workout clothes and meet her on the lawn.

"I thought you'd quit as my trainer," he chided.

"I said I'd quit if you slept with those girls."

"How do you know I didn't?"

"Because you're not that stupid."

"Look," said Jesse, "I'll be back in a few minutes. I've got to catch up with Walter." He went to the door.

"Where are you going?" I asked.

He felt in his pocket for his wallet. "We should tell your friend Bonita about her car. I want to give Paul a call."

By the look on his face both Tina and I knew that he wasn't concerned about Bonita and her car. He was worried about what was happening at home. He took off down the laneway.

"Tina," I said, "I want to call Dad."

"Forget it."

"Aren't you wondering how he's doing?"

"No."

CHAPTER SIXTEEN

"Almost there," said Walter, turning his head so he could holler out the window of the pick-up truck.

We would have made it to our destination sooner, but it took the twins half the day to get ready. Tina and I tried to persuade them to stay home, reminding them that it was only a junkyard we were going to, and since we had to come back to put the new rad in Brandy, they would have another whole night to tinker with Jesse.

There was no talking them out of joining us, however, due to the fact that very close to the junkyard was a bar called The Thirsty Cactus that had music and dancing. Tina said we had no time for that crap, but Walter wanted to try the place out, and since he was helping us by fixing up Brandy, we didn't have much choice.

It didn't seem right that Jesse got to ride up front with Walter while Darlene, Charlene, Tina and I got stuck in the bed of the truck, especially when it was so danger-ous. There was nothing dangerous about the truck itself; although it was rusty and looked as if it had been created from the remains of cars, trucks, motorcycles and boats, I fully trusted Walter's skills in automobile maintenance.

The real danger lay in putting Tina and Darlene in a moving vehicle, when both would have loved nothing more than to push the other one out. Walter said that putting Jesse back there with the twins would be more of a hazard, so we agreed to the seating arrangement.

We were about halfway to our destination, when we drove through a small, two-light town and had to stop for gas. The service station was next to a high school, and Tina spotted a couple of runners doing laps on the track. She banged on the cab window behind Jesse's head.

"Get out, Mankiller," she hollered.

"What are you talking about?" he asked her.

"I said get out." She crawled out the gate of the truck and opened the door beside him.

"You can't go a whole day without training," she insisted. "Judd Stone's getting ready to kill you as we speak." She shielded her eyes with the back of her hand and watched as the runners raced by. "Okay, so you're going to lap those two guys right there."

"In jeans?" he said.

"In your shorts."

"Whatever you say," said Jesse, undoing his belt with a dramatic sweep.

Darlene smiled and fixed her eyes on his jeans. Charlene bit her bottom lip in anticipation.

"Not those shorts, you idiot," hollered Tina. She threw him a pair of sports trunks. He leaned against the side of the truck, let his jeans drop and put them on. The twins hung over the side of the bed to watch.

"You think of everything," I said.

"I want him to win."

As the six of us made our way to the track, I had a chance to talk to Tina privately.

"Why do you care so much about Jesse winning?" I asked her.

She didn't answer. Just pulled a blade of grass out of the ground, held it between her thumbs and made a sound like a goose call by blowing on it. Then she told Jesse to start pacing the other runners.

Walter, Tina, the twins and I sat on a bench beside the track.

"Not like that, Mankiller," she screamed, when he started making his way around the circle.

He threw his arms in the air as if to say, "What the hell do you want?"

That's when she told him to do it backwards. "It's the only way to build foot speed and awareness in the ring," Tina told Walter, who looked to me like he hadn't run or even walked two miles in his entire life.

"Right," he said, pulling a package of candy from his back pocket and passing it around.

Dar and Char should have had pom-poms. They cheered in high-pitched unison and jumped up and down when Jesse flew past the other joggers backward, taking big energetic strides. His calves were clearly burning as he dug his feet into the track, and he worked up such a sweat that his clothes were completely soaked by the time Tina told him he could stop.

He loped over to where we were sitting and bent over with both hands on his knees until his breath came back.

"Now you owe me, Tina," said Jesse.

"I don't owe you anything."

"One wish."

"Forget it."

"And if I can go around a second time, two wishes," he said, making his way back to the track.

He stopped. "Let's make it three," he hollered.

Jesse proceeded to push his body to the limit and actually did it three more times. Backward.

"Put that in your smipe and poke it," he told Tina, who was grinning because she now knew that he had the endurance necessary to go the distance in the ring. And for some reason, unforeseen to me but obvious to my sister, she was determined that Jesse Mankiller would be the next light-heavyweight champion of the world.

—

We made it to Fenton Mills in about two hours, and it was a bumpy ride in more ways than one. It was already late in the day by the time we got to the junkyard, and Walter was so entranced by the place, he spent at least another hour – as wide-eyed as a girl trying to choose her first prom dress – picking out carburetors, tailpipes and distributor caps. Once we'd purchased the rad, and once Walter'd had a chance to complete his junkyard tour for other parts for other projects (which almost filled the back of his truck and made it nearly impossible for us to fit in again for the ride home), we headed to the Cactus.

Fenton Mills was one of those towns where if you were in a coma for a few years and suddenly woke up, you would know immediately what day of the week it was. Friday night meant that pick-up trucks gathered around The Thirsty Cactus like rhinos around a watering hole, so Walter's rig was right at home with the others when we pulled into the lot. Darlene and Charlene jumped out like two spaniels ready to hunt, while I slid out over the back bumper.

"I'll wait here," said my sister, making herself at home between a bucket seat and an outboard motor.

"Oh, come on," I said. "It'll be fun."

"I don't want to." She leaned back and put her feet on the tailgate.

"Do what you want," I said. Then under my breath added, "You will anyway."

I followed Walter and Jesse into the Cactus; Jesse still hadn't dried completely, but his sweat blended in nicely with the other men in the bar, most of whom had set out for the place when the whistle blew at five, without going home for a shower.

The twins had already managed to cajole the bartender into giving over two gin and tonics despite the fact they were underaged. Walter and Jesse each had a draught beer and got me an orange soda. (Once I'd finished it, Walter kindly poured some of his beer into my glass; if he hadn't drunk half of it first, it would have tasted better.)

"Where's Tina?" Jesse asked, his eyes panning the bar.

"She's not coming," I said.

"Why is Tina going to Boston anyway?" he asked.

"I can't tell you that."

"You could, but you won't."

"You'll have to ask her yourself," I said, knowing that he had about as much chance of dragging that out of her as Ellwood did of watching *Gunsmoke*.

"Why won't she join us?" asked Walter.

"She doesn't like public places much," I admitted. "Except boxing arenas."

"Good," chirped Darlene.

"Yeah," added Charlene with a blink.

"That's not very nice," said Walter, signalling to the waitress for another beer for Jesse and ordering a plate of fries, wings and some deep-fried cheese balls. His excuse was that he was driving, so he'd better eat and not drink, but I figured those deep-fried cheese balls would have been his first choice even if we were all going home on the bus.

"Tina won't be too happy if you have more than one beer," I warned Jesse, but that only made him chug back the second one out of spite. A band was setting up their instruments not far from us, and they were clearing a dance floor in the middle of the place. Unfortunately it was a country and western band; I could tell from the banjo and the fringes on the lead singer's shirt. That and the fact they warmed up with "Mama, Don't Let Your Babies Grow up to be Cowboys."

I imagined myself dancing with Jesse anyway – his muscular arms around my waist – and all the girls in the place turning green with envy. Already they were gawking at him, watching his every move. And then suddenly, without warning, their heads turned toward the door and they were staring at someone else.

It was Tina.

She waltzed in the door with two guys – two big burly guys in red plaid jackets and leather boots laced only half way and once-white-but-now-grey baseball caps. The kind of guys who have a vocabulary of five words and four of them are dirty. They were arguing, and I heard her say something about two hundred dollars. They argued some more, and she changed it to fifty.

Jesse turned around in his chair to see what was going on.

Tina and the two guys headed straight to the pool table. While they racked up the balls, my sister went behind the bar, found a stool and pushed it over to the table.

"Nine ball?"

"Right," said one of the guys, handing her a cue.

Tina took a square of chalk off the holder, then stood next to the cue to see if it was regulation length. It was a good ten inches taller than she was.

"This is a snooker cue," she hollered. "Too long for pool. What – you think I wouldn't notice?"

One of the guys went to the rack and returned with another cue, which she proceeded to chalk up.

I headed to the pool table and asked her how she met these two and got them suckered into a game.

"Not now, Ellie," she said, lining up her shot. "Seven ball, corner pocket," she declared, and *Wham!* in it went, just as she said it would.

I returned to the table, and by then the band was playing. I'd hoped Jesse would ask me to dance, but he didn't. He just sat there, staring into space. I figured he was thinking about his sister. Every once in a while, his gaze landed at the pool table where Tina continued to sink balls. Slowly but surely, more and more people gathered around to watch.

Darlene's eyes looked like two little gin and tonics as she burped behind her hand then slithered around the table and draped her arms over Jesse's neck. I was hoping she wasn't going to do that "Boo!" thing again. She didn't. This time she pulled him out of the chair and insisted he dance with her.

Jesse was an excellent dancer. He moved with the music effortlessly. I don't know if it was because he'd had a couple of beers or if he was just born with a natural sense of rhythm, but even though he was a Bruce Springsteen fan (a fact I discerned from the hundreds of times he'd changed radio stations so he could hear "Born to Run"), he had no problem dancing to country and western music. Darlene didn't either and she squealed in delight when he grabbed her hand and swung her around. Once, when it was one of the burly guys' turn at the pool table, I caught Tina watching Jesse too.

I knew that despite being in the process of killing two men at nine-ball, her normally-impossible-to-attract-unless-it's-boxing-related attention was attracted by Jesse's smooth moves. She snapped up her cue, gave it another dose of chalk (I think she was pretending the end of the stick was Darlene's nose) and proceeded to sink every ball on the table.

Darlene managed to hang on to Jesse through two Conway Twitty songs, a Glen Campbell and a Kenny Rogers. I knew she was holding out for a slow dance, so when the band finally played one, I watched as her long, pink nails grew into points and held him firmly in her grasp.

Jesse broke away from her though. In my fantasy, he came back to the table, reached for my hand and pulled me to the dance floor. In fact, he marched right past our table (Charlene stood up and blinked, thinking he was coming for her) then made a beeline to the pool tables, whispered something into my sister's ear and plucked her off the stool.

She whacked him over the head with the cue, but then it slipped from her grip and dropped somewhere between the two burly guys and the dance floor.

She hollered something about putting her down or she'd be out fifty bucks.

She screamed something about letting her go or else.

She told him that she never dances under any circumstances.

He whispered in her ear again.

"Stick your three wishes," said Tina. "I'm not your goddamn fairy godmother."

She was right. She wasn't anybody's fairy godmother. But when Jesse grabbed her, pulled her as close to his chest as he possibly could, leaned over her without giving a damn about their height difference and forced her to dance, she was the closest thing to Cinderella at the ball I'd ever seen in my life.

CHAPTER SEVENTEEN

Saying good-bye to the Valentines was a bit like standing up when the credits roll at the end of a movie. On the one hand, you're happy to be stretching your legs and brushing off the bits of popcorn that have fallen into your lap, but on the other, when the bright lights go on over your head and the imaginary world in which you were living evaporates like mist in the sun, you can't help but experience a sense of being tossed back unceremoniously into the real world. That's what it felt like when we pulled out of the Valentines' driveway.

Dar and Char had made one last attempt at capturing Jesse. They chose several pairs of their prettiest underthings and – once they were certain he was watching – proceeded to hang them on the clothesline, one by one and with such aplomb I thought it might actually work, and Jesse would leave the world of boxing, join Walter and Ellwood in their endeavor to raise chickens and reconstruct cars and marry Darlene. Or Charlene. Or both – no one would be the wiser behind all those trees.

I think the girls' final attempt would have been more successful had Ellwood not joined them at the clothesline with a laundry basket full of his underwear – grey, torn and stained. Due to the situation with their well, all clothes had to be done in the pond, so there was even some algae dripping off the fly front.

Walter refused to take any payment for his work on Brandy, claiming that it was an honour to work on so fine a vehicle. He wondered, though, if he could keep the old rad, saying it was "about as useful as a milk pail under a bull," but he'd like to have it as a souvenir. Despite the fact that he looked like he was molded from dough, I liked Walter. He was a good guy with a good heart, and I truly hoped his life would work out for the best.

We didn't see Dot when we departed – it was too early in the day – but she left an envelope for Tina to take to Hollywood. It was addressed to Johnny Carson and marked personal and confidential.

Tina went to tear it into pieces, but I suggested we save it as one of those time capsule things that we open up in ten years for a laugh. She must have tossed it out the window somewhere between the Valentines' and Boston, or maybe it got left in one of the boxing arenas along our route or misplaced at one of the motels, but it was never seen again.

—

Our map described Portland as "a picturesque seaside city full of Victorian charm and classic Maine style." That may have been so, but our motel was nowhere near the ocean, had about as much charm as the two burly guys Tina had beat at pool and the only view was the back entrance of the arena where Jesse's fight was going to take place the following night.

Both Jesse and Tina were unnervingly quiet during the drive to Portland. Jesse kept one arm draped over the wheel and stared straight ahead at the road. I figured he was thinking about Meryl again; he'd made another call and had learned that his sister was nowhere to be found. That, in turn, messed up Tina's mind, because she knew that even the slightest distraction could destroy his chance of beating Judd Stone.

Tina didn't say what else was bothering her, but the closer we got to Boston, the larger Count Ilizarov loomed, and that was a bitter reality neither one of us could ignore. I hadn't forgotten my promise to Azalea that I would try to talk her out of the whole thing; I was waiting for the right moment when she might be more reasonable and open to seeing things my way. But waiting for a moment for Tina to be reasonable and open to seeing things anybody's way was like trying to dash across the road at rush hour. Wait too long and you'll be there forever. Attempt to cross too soon and you'll be smashed to pieces.

It was dark by the time we'd had some supper and checked into our room at the Flamingo Motel. Other than the fact that it was pink, I saw no good reason for the name, and when I asked the attendant, who didn't speak English, she just smiled, nodded her head and assured me that whatever happens in the Flamingo, stays in the Flamingo.

Tina and I had just crawled into our bed (still dressed, as usual), and Jesse had collapsed into his – the poor guy had been driving all day, and Tina made him work on combinations after that – when we heard a knock at our door. I knew right off the bat that it wasn't a friendly knock. Friendly knocks are *rap a tap tap*. This was more like one big *thud*.

"Don't answer it," I said.

"Don't be ridiculous," said Tina.

"Who is it?" hollered Jesse, pulling off his cover and reaching for a pair of sweats. (Oh, how Dar and Char would have loved it.)

Another *thud*.

Jesse opened the door and the two creeps who'd threatened us in Amherst – the blond and the ugly one – barged in and rammed a pistol into Jesse's face.

I started to shake uncontrollably.

"Sit down, Ellie, and keep quiet," blurted Tina. Then her voice changed, and she calmly suggested to our visitors that they needn't do that, that Jesse was willing to talk.

"Like hell I am," said Jesse, so they threw him against the wall.

"Don't be an ass, Mankiller. Leave this to me."

"We are here to bring you a little word of advice," said the ugly one. "You are going to take a dive tomorrow night, and it is going to happen in the third round. For your troubles, Mr. Mankiller, we are going to give you five thousand bucks."

"Which is more than you are worth," added his sidekick.

"I'm not going down for—"

The blond shoved the barrel of another gun right into his neck.

"We will see you tomorrow night," said Tina.

Jesse thought she was giving in.

"I'm not—"

Tina stopped him. "We'll see you tomorrow night," she repeated, and they drew back their guns and muscled out the door. But not before blondie warned us once again that if Jesse didn't comply and take a fall for the mob, he would wind up in that picturesque harbour we'd heard so much about. And I could tell by the way he said it that I was probably heading there too.

Tina locked the door behind them, turned off the light and went back to bed.

Jesse and I looked at each other. Then he spoke to Tina.

"I'm not throwing the fight, you know."

"Of course you're not."

"I think we should call the police," I said.

"Police?" scoffed Tina. "And tell them what? That we were threatened by the mob?" She snickered. "What are they going to do, Ellie? Ask them to stop?"

That's when I saw my life flash before me like a movie and heard the offstage sound effect of three coffin lids slamming shut.

—

The crowd at the Portland arena was the biggest one Jesse had ever fought in front of. And it was like nothing Tina and I had ever seen either.

She never mentioned the threats and carried on as usual, going over her plans and giving Jesse her best advice as to how to beat the hell out of Judd Stone.

"He's a brawler," she told him. "I know how this guy fights. He lacks finesse and footwork, but his punch is like being hit by a Mack Truck."

Jesse nodded. Already there was sweat dripping down his face.

"He lacks mobility, Mankiller, and that's where you have the advantage. His punches are powerful, there's no denying it. But he's slow enough to be predictable, and I think if you're on your toes, you can see them coming. That's what you've got to do. Then, when he leaves himself open, you use that uppercut of yours and he's history."

Jesse nodded again.

We were just about to head down the stairs and into the arena when our two friends, the cutthroats, blocked our path. Only this time there were four of them.

"What's your decision?"

"Outta my way," said Tina.

What's she doing? She's going to get us killed.

One of them turned to Jesse. "You'd think you'd be back home by now. Your sister the way she is."

Jesse flew into a rage. "What the hell do you know about my sister?" He reached for the guy's neck, but one of the other thugs stuck a gun in Jesse's back.

"She tried to send herself west. Slit her wrist, that's what we heard."

Jesse's eyes circulated between the men, Tina and the stadium.

"I'm outta here," he said, and went to take off.

"Like hell you are," screamed Tina. She ran after him, grabbed his robe and held it tight. "They're just trying to freak you out. Make you lose your cool so you can't fight."

I was the one freaking out. "Let's go, Tina," I said, looking back at the thugs who were slowly tucking their guns into their holsters while watching us closely. "Let's go home. Let's forget about your operation." Tears flowed down my cheeks and my heart felt like it had dropped out the bottom of my chest.

"Shut up," said Tina. "Just shut up."

I realized I'd let the cat out of the bag.

Jesse broke free of Tina. I hoped he hadn't heard the part about the operation, but I was pretty sure he had.

Tina grabbed him again. "These goons are just yanking your chain, Jesse. This is your chance, for you and for your sister. Don't throw it away."

She let him go.

He turned to leave, then he stopped.

He stared at the ground for what seemed like a year. Then he walked over to the four mobsters and told them he was going to fight Stone and he was going to win.

That's when they pulled out a semi-automatic and pushed him out the exit door.

CHAPTER EIGHTEEN

"Oh, for God's sake," said Tina, following them into the alley.

For God's sake? We're about to get liquidated, and that's your response?

I didn't know what to do. If I followed her outside I could be murdered on the spot. If I took off for safety, she could be murdered and I'd have no way of identifying which one did it.

"Are you coming, Ellie?" I heard her holler from outside. "I could use your help for a minute."

Use my help for a minute? She made it sound like she was wrapping a present and needed me to stick my finger in the ribbon so she could tie a bow.

I opened the exit door just a crack and peered outside to the parking lot.

Tina and Jesse were pushed up against the Jaguar, and one of the creeps was busy fitting a silencer on the end of his Beretta.

Tina saw my eye. "Get the hell out here. Now!"

I crept slowly through the door.

"Will you tell these *gentlemen* who my friend is, El-lie?"

"Friend?"

"Oh, God," she hissed. "Mickey! Mickey O'Shea!"

"Yes. Yes, that's right. She and him are good friends," I said with a gulp. Then I twisted two fingers together. "They're like that."

Jesse didn't say a word. Standing there in his trunks and robe, a couple of guns in his face, he watched in fascination as Tina talked down the mobsters.

But the blond wasn't having any of it and signalled the ugly guy to shove Jesse into the trunk of the Jag.

Oh my God. It's all over for us.

Just then a car pulled up and rolled to a stop beside us. It was a metallic silver Maserati with Québec plates.

The door opened slowly, the driver reached for a jacket that was draped over the passenger seat, then he got out and let the door close itself. It locked automatically, and when I heard the click, I jumped, thinking somebody had pulled their trigger.

Is that Mickey O'Shea?

"Tina!" he said, smiling widely and greeting her like she was family and we were all at a picnic. He grasped both her shoulders and squeezed them in a hug-like gesture. Maybe it was a special mobster hug. Then he held up his hand so the banditos would put away their guns.

"Thanks for coming, Mickey," said Tina.

Thanks for coming?

"That's all right. I was going to stop here to watch Stone anyway." He checked his watch. "Looks like I made it just in time."

You can say that again.

"This is the mysterious call you made from the restaurant?" asked Jesse.

Tina didn't answer, just continued chatting with O'Shea. They carried on like a couple of old ladies who finally got through on the party line and weren't going to be interrupted for anyone.

"So, you see why this means so much to me and why I need you to call these guys off."

"Okay, look," he said. "I haven't got a fortune riding on this fight, nothing like that. I'm going to let this one go, for you." He paused. "For *you*, Tina, because I like you. Okay? I know the kind of crap life has thrown at you."

Thank God he liked her. Thank God life had thrown crap at her.

"Thank you," said my sister.

"But next time I'm in the Pier, you owe me a few beers, right?"

She smiled at him.

"And I can watch you beat the hell out of some losers at pool."

"You've got it," said Tina.

"So that was all made up crap about my sister?" Jesse asked O'Shea.

"I don't know anything about your sister."

His henchmen didn't answer. Oddly, I had the feeling that maybe – and I hated to think it – maybe they weren't making it up and maybe Meryl was in trouble.

"Okay, slugger," said O'Shea, slapping Jesse on the back, "let's see what you can do." He smirked. "Just because I'm letting this one go, doesn't mean you're going to beat Stone, you realize that. This isn't going to be a walk in the park. Frankly, I think he's going to kill you."

—

Jesse and Stone settled right into a grinding fight. The crowd was loud, obnoxious and out for blood. Not everyone was on Judd Stone's side, but he had the majority and Jesse knew it. He was forced to endure some nasty racial slurs from his opponent's camp, which he did with dignity and style.

I was proud of Jesse and the way he kept up the pressure on Stone for the first round. Still, he was going to need to build some combinations – something to throw Stone off his balance. Jesse's jabs were crisp, but Stone, who had a thick, square neck and stumpy legs like tree trunks, avoided most of them, and even when Jesse connected, it was like trying to knock down a Neanderthal.

Between rounds, Tina hollered at Jesse while I cleaned him up. "What's wrong with you, Mankiller? You're going to be dead meat in the next ten minutes if you don't get your act together, do you hear me? Jab, jab, hook – right?"

He heard her, but the next two rounds were the same. He dodged every hook, but Stone kept plodding after him, with slow, heavy feet that reminded me of sasquatch. After the third round, Tina urged Jesse to take him out with a short right uppercut to his massive jaw. Jesse nodded, but Tina felt that he needed a push to get things moving, so as he was getting ready to head back into the ring, she scooped up a handful of ice from our bucket, pulled open the front of his shorts, and tossed it in there like she was feeding fish at Marineland.

He swore at her, and she swore back, but the bell rang just in time; otherwise, the two of them would have become the main attraction. The ice kept Jesse moving at first, but not long enough, and Stone bullied him around the ring and got him into the perfect position for a significant left hook.

Wham! Jesse fell back against the ropes. He stumbled up and forward toward Stone, who got him again, this time with a right cross.

Jesse was down. And he was in pain – massive rope burns across his back made it look like he'd been lashed.

The referee started the count.

Tina was screaming at Jesse to get up.

Everyone in the arena was hollering too, catcalls that burned my ears and whistles that were so high-pitched they could penetrate even Tina's skull. Then suddenly they stopped and the place went silent when Jesse got up. Barely.

The doctor rushed over to examine him.

"Who are you fighting?"

"Judd Stone."

"What city are you in?"

"Portland."

The doctor was almost finished when someone from Stone's camp decided to hurl an insult at Tina. And it was no paltry little sticks-and-stones-may-break-my-bones kind of insult. It was straight from hell.

"Too bad, Mankiller," said Stone's cornerman, "but that's what you get when you hire a manager from Oz." A bunch of idiots started laughing hysterically.

I hoped Tina hadn't heard, but she did. The expression on her face broke my heart.

I think it broke Jesse's too, because when the doctor allowed the fight to continue, he jumped up, threw his towel clear across the ring and came at Stone like he was avenging a murder.

A cocky, grinning Stone sauntered back into the ring, basking in the cheers from the screaming crowd and throwing kisses like he'd already won. That was when Jesse pinned him with several quick uppercuts to the chin and heavy punishing rights to his body. He topped it off with a beautiful looping left hook – sharp, short and on the mark – and knocked Stone out cold. Stone cold.

That knockout earned Jesse more money than he could make in a year anyplace else, meant that he was the new holder of the American title and assured him that he would go to Boston for the North American crown.

—

Jesse was in no shape to celebrate; having taken so much abuse in the first few rounds, he was dazed and exhausted. He answered some brief questions for sports reporters, but the physician took him aside to treat his rope burns and examine his swellings and contusions. Then he warned him to rest.

"Why didn't *you* talk to those reporters?" he asked Tina when we were back at the motel. He slumped into a chair and held an ice pack to his face.

"I have nothing to say. Your performance speaks for itself."

"You've disappeared after every fight," Jesse muttered.

I explained why. "Our father follows the sports pages religiously. She doesn't want him to know she's your manager." I glanced at Tina. "It's a good thing these fights haven't been televised."

"Jesse'll be on the tube soon enough." Tina threw herself down on the bed. "You make it to the Boston Garden in September and I guarantee that one will be broadcast right across North America."

"Won't this next fight be televised?" I asked my sister.

"It might be," she admitted. "I hope not."

"Why do you care if Dad knows?"

She didn't answer me and spoke to Jesse instead. "Are you well enough to call Paul, or do you want me to do it for you? He'd probably like to get the news from you – if he hasn't heard it on the radio already."

"I can do it," said Jesse. "I have to talk to him anyway."

"Don't be long," warned my sister. "You need sleep."

While Jesse went to use the motel phone, Tina decided to take a shower. The lock on the door was broken, and there was no way she'd take her clothes off if there was even a remote chance of Jesse walking in, so she made me wait inside the bathroom and guard the door like it was the back of an armoured truck.

It seemed like an eternity, but when she finally finished her shower, I decided to have one myself, while Tina brushed her teeth and used the ancient little, low-powered, built-in hairdryer. The water was lukewarm, brown and only one step up from the Valentines' pond, but when you've been spattered with blood and sweat and spit, anything will do.

It must have been half an hour by the time we came out, and we were anxious to hear from Jesse what Paul had to say about his remarkable win. But Jesse wasn't there.

Instead, Mickey O'Shea was sitting on the edge of the bed.

"Got some bad news," he said, lighting a cigarette and searching the drawers for an ashtray. "Yeah, really bad news."

CHAPTER NINETEEN

"What are you talking about?" cried Tina. "Where's Jesse?"

I pulled open the door and checked the parking lot. Brandy was there, but Jesse was not. I glared at O'Shea.

"Listen, Tina," said O'Shea, calmly and between two drags of his cigarette, "my boys had nothing to do with this." He looked at me. "What's your name again?"

"Ellie."

"Where is he?" asked Tina.

"He called somebody – in Halifax, I think – and what my boys told him was right. His sister is in bad shape."

"What are you saying? That he's gone back to Truro?" hollered Tina.

"That's what I'm saying." O'Shea nodded his head.

"What? You've got to be kidding me. Tell me you're kidding me."

"Well, you can't blame Jesse for worrying about his sister," I said.

O'Shea agreed. "I offered the kid a drive to Nova Scotia. I'm headed that way. But he asked me to take you to Boston instead. What's happening in Boston?"

Tina didn't answer him.

"I don't mind doing Mankiller a favour," said O'Shea, "but you know how I am about favours—"

Tina cut him off mid sentence, grabbed her purse and yanked open the door. "We've got to find Jesse before he gets too far. Maybe your Maserati would be faster than our car."

"Oh, yeah," said O'Shea, "it's faster. That's why I loaned it to your friend."

"You did what?" hollered Tina. "He's in no shape to drive. He could collapse at the wheel any moment!"

"He's not stupid, right?" said O'Shea. "He'll stop somewhere to sleep."

"No, he won't," replied Tina. "Why'd you let him take your car? What's in it for you? He won't throw a fight, I know that for sure."

"I know that too," said O'Shea. "Maybe I'm just a nice guy, okay?"

I doubt it, I said to myself.

"Come on," shouted Tina. "We've got to catch up with him. Somehow."

We tossed our luggage back into Brandy and hit the main highway. Tina got O'Shea to drive so fast that the neon signs from service stations, truck stops and motels became one long blurry ribbon of light.

"The way he's bleeding, it's a wonder you let him in your car," said Tina, her eyes fixed on the highway ahead.

I don't imagine blood disturbs him very much, I thought, taking a good long look at the mob boss behind the wheel. You could tell from the way he dressed that O'Shea was a Montrealer. Despite being a notorious criminal, he had excellent taste and was beyond cool. Not just his Maserati or his leather jacket; his whole demeanor, even the way he combed his hair was cool. Driving with him in Brandy, however, was like hiring James Bond to help you track down a chicken thief.

O'Shea looked at the huge chrome dashboard. "Whose boat is this anyway?"

"I borrowed it from a friend."

Tina thought for a minute. "Now I get it. You were happy to give Jesse your car because you don't want him to fight in Boston. Right? You think I'm stupid? Sure, send him back to Truro in a Maserati, half crazy from being hit in the head, so he'll kill himself. Your car's insured."

"Hey, Tina, hear me out. I've got nothing on that fight in Boston now that Stone's out of the match." He swerved to avoid a pothole.

I'm not sure if Tina believed him or not, but she insisted that we keep driving, all the way back to Truro, if necessary. She was bound and determined that Jesse would fight.

"That kid's a real contender," admitted O'Shea. He had his elbow out the window and was driving way too fast for my taste. "I'd like to get him on my side."

"Won't happen," said Tina. "He's too proud for any kind of deals. Anyway, I thought you were after Ryan Byrne."

"I'm not sure about him," admitted O'Shea, and Tina nodded in agreement.

"Well he's Dad's best hope, so I'm rooting for him," I said.

While we sailed down the highway and the two of them rattled on about boxing, I started to listen in fascinated horror to the sound of my own thoughts. *What if O'Shea had knocked off Jesse for winning that fight against Stone? What if he had him chained in a basement someplace? What if he didn't really loan his car to Jesse but had murdered him instead and was simply buying time by driving us back to Canada? What if he was taking Tina and me to some hideout where we, too, would be executed, and he was using Brandy as his getaway car?*

"Tina?" I said, my voice creaking like an old rocking chair.

"What is it, Ellie?"

"I'm really tired. We've been up for eighteen hours now. Can't we find a motel or something?"

"Sleep back there," she barked.

"Yeah, but…."

"But what?"

"Mr. O'Shea must be tired too. We really shouldn't be driving like this, in the dead of night when we're all bone tired." I didn't know if criminals ever slept but hoped O'Shea would at least want to rest for a couple hours.

He didn't. It wasn't until we veered onto the shoulder a couple of times that Tina realized she was pushing us too hard and that we had to find someplace to sleep. The only problem was that we were out in the middle of nowhere, miles from Portland, miles from any town and miles from the Canadian border.

The only place we weren't miles from was the Valentines'.

—

The house was in darkness except for the glow of a television from the living room. We figured it was Dot watching *The Tonight Show*.

She opened the door when we knocked, but rather than greeting us – she couldn't because her mouth was full and she couldn't leave Johnny Carson – she waved us in, pointed to a plate of donuts (that had obviously come out of a freezer because they were beaded with moisture) and threw herself back down in front of the set.

When O'Shea, a man whom she'd never met in her life, sat down next to her, she didn't even bat an eye, despite being clothed in a big caftan with huge armholes and a low neck that – whenever she reached for a donut or leaned back on the couch – displayed several of her body parts clearly.

He didn't seem to care either, and the two of them laughed hysterically at Carson's jokes (which I didn't find especially funny) and sang along with Barbara Streisand when she did "People. People who need people, Are the luckiest people in the world. People. People who need people…."

At a commercial break, Dot asked Tina if she had the letter for Johnny with her. She wanted to read it, make sure it was right. When Tina lied and told her she'd "lost" it, Dot waddled over to a desk, took out a pad, and started writing another one. I noticed a half-completed needle-point sitting on the desk; it was quite colourful and the border was comprised of flowers and vines. I picked it up to admire it and asked Dot if she was the one who had done it.

"Yes," she said, "that's my work. Keeps me happy. Keeps me from getting blue." Then she pointed to one in a frame on the wall. It had a floral theme also, with a biblical verse in the middle: "Be not forgetful to entertain strangers, for thereby some have entertained angels unawares." I looked over at Mickey, and thought to myself that entertaining strangers can go either way.

Tina and I made our way to the guest room and left Dot with Mickey and Johnny. I was completely exhausted and nothing would have stopped me from falling asleep. Tina couldn't though, and she kept me up for an hour, filling my mind with all the terrible things that could happen to Jesse.

"That idiot will try to get back to Truro tonight … Maserati … two hundred miles an hour … nothing to eat … almost knocked out in the third round … no sleep … eighteen hours."

Her sentences floated through my mind, along with the lyrics to "People," and I drifted in and out of consciousness until finally my body couldn't take it anymore and I fell sound asleep.

When I woke up, Tina was already downstairs and eating cereal with Ellwood. Darlene and Charlene were in the barn trying to find where we'd hidden Jesse, Dot was in bed, Walter was starting to take Brandy apart and Mickey O'Shea was sound asleep on the living room couch.

"Found him there this morning," said Ellwood, pouring me a generous helping of corn flakes. "Didn't recognize him, so I figured he must have wandered in from the highway." He pushed a carton of milk across the table. "Then your sister here said he'd come with you." He paused to scratch the back of his head. "What happened to that nice young Indian fellow you had with you the last time?"

"He's got a problem at home in Nova Scotia," I said.

"That's too bad," said Ellwood. "Too bad."

Mickey woke up when he heard us talking.

"Set yourself down," said Ellwood, "and have a bowl of cereal."

Mickey declined, choosing to smoke instead. He checked his watch a few times, which we took as a hint that he wanted to get going.

"What's that?" I asked him, noticing a large manila envelope in his hand.

"An autographed photograph of Carson," he said. "Dot gave it to me." He looked at Tina, then at me. "Nice, eh?"

"I'm surprised she parted with it," said Tina.

Ellwood wasn't surprised. "She's got fourteen of those things."

We were on our way out the door – luckily, Walter hadn't gotten too far with Brandy and put everything back in place quickly – when Dot came down to say good-bye. Still in her nightgown and half asleep, she managed to stumble out and stop us before we got away so she could give Tina the new letter.

"Yeah, whatever," replied Tina, when Dot wished her luck in Hollywood.

"Hollywood?" inquired O'Shea, once we'd pulled out of the driveway.

"Don't ask," said Tina, ripping up the letter and letting the little pieces fly out the window in every direction.

A few miles down the road, I noticed that Tina seemed much calmer than she had the night before. She wasn't hanging out the window, screaming Jesse's name anymore. I asked her why.

"I suspect that he's been incarcerated by now and some jailhouse physician is looking after him."

"What makes you say that?" asked O'Shea.

"Think about it. A Native guy, nineteen years old, with a long braid down the middle of his back, covered with blood and bruises, is driving a Maserati down a well-policed highway at top speed in the middle of the night. How far do you think he'd get?"

CHAPTER TWENTY

Turns out Jesse did make it back to Truro that night. We found him in the waiting room of the hospital, his head down and half a dozen empty coffee cups scattered beside him.

"Jesse!" said Tina, tossing her suitcase onto the nearest seat.

"Are you okay?" I asked him.

His head came up slowly. He had dried blood stuck to his forehead and cheeks. He said nothing.

"Your sister … is she …?" Tina couldn't find the words.

"She's all right." He put his head down.

"Where's your mother?" I wondered.

"With my aunt. They sent her home."

"Can they get your sister some kind of help?" asked Tina. "Counselling or something?"

"They will. I guess."

"Well, then you should be at home asleep," scolded Tina. "There's nothing you can do here."

"I'm not leaving." He looked over the empty cups to find one with something left in it; he tilted it up and drank the dregs. Then he tossed the keys to the Maserati to O'Shea. "Thanks, man," he mumbled.

"Tina said you'd be stopped at the border," said O'Shea. "What did you do? Bribe the guard?"

"Just told him the truth." Jesse lowered his head again, then muttered something about the guy being a boxing fan.

"Mankiller," said O'Shea, "you are one hell of a fighter. I mean that. Your manager here" – he gestured toward Tina – "now she isn't interested in my way of doing things. But if you ever change your mind…."

"He won't," said Tina. "But listen, Mickey," she added, "the three of us are really grateful for your help. I owe you big time."

"Good luck," he said, throwing his jacket over his shoulder and waving with his keys between his fingers.

Paul and Bonita walked through the door just as O'Shea was walking out. Paul recognized him and did a double take.

"Tina! Ellie!" Bonita gave us both a big hug. "You guys are amazing. I can't get over it." She looked at Jesse. "Oh, but I'm sorry about your sister. Really, I am. I didn't mean to sound upbeat. But you did so well in Amherst and Portland. I can't believe it." She put a hand on Jesse's shoulder. "And they say your sister is going to be just fine."

"Bonita's right," echoed Paul. "Meryl will be looked after. You can be sure of that." He walked over to Tina. "That wasn't Mickey O'Shea, was it?"

"Yeah, he drove us back. It's a long story."

Paul shrugged. "Well, you are a remarkable young lady."

Tina changed the subject. "How are you, Paul? Will your doctors let you get back to being a manager?"

"No, unfortunately not. My days in boxing are over. It's back to teaching physical education for me." He smiled at Jesse. "You've got a great career ahead of you, though."

"I don't think so." Jesse crushed his cup it in his hand.

"You are a fool," said Tina. "An absolute fool. And I am sick and tired of having to give you pep talks. You know that if you return to Boston and you win that fight, you'll be in the world circuit. You will be able to buy your mom a house to live in and she won't have to be wheeled up a plywood plank."

Jesse looked daggers at my sister.

"I'm sorry to be so blunt, but you're stubborn, and it's the only way to deal with you sometimes."

"Most of the time," said Paul.

Jesse looked daggers at him too.

"Even if you don't win," added Bonita, "just stepping into the ring should bring you a fair bit of money."

"Enough to help your mother and sisters." Tina sat down next to Jesse. "Isn't it what your father would have wanted? Isn't it exactly what he would have done?" She folded both arms in front. "Okay, Mankiller. I'm done begging. The rest is up to you."

Jesse lifted his head. One of his cuts had reopened, and my sister took some tissues from her purse and pressed them against it.

"Hand me the salve," she told me. "It's in my luggage, in the zippered pocket."

Tina fixed up his cuts.

Then Jesse looked her straight in the eye. "Why are you going to Boston?" he asked. "It's for some kind of operation, isn't it?"

Tina turned crimson red.

Bonita had the good sense to ask Paul if he'd like to join her for a coffee in the cafeteria, and I moved to the next row of seats and picked up a magazine to give my sister an opportunity to confide in Jesse.

"Yes, it is."

"What for?"

"I don't like talking about it."

"I don't like talking about my problems, either," said Jesse, "but that doesn't stop you from … well, it doesn't stop you."

Tina knew he was right. She took a deep breath, paused for a minute, then finally answered his question. "The Ilizarov procedure," she said.

He squinted as if to say "what the hell is that?"

"It's to make me taller, okay?" I peered over the top of the magazine and saw that Tina was in tears. She wiped her eyes with the blood-soaked tissues she'd used on Jesse's cuts, smearing his blood across her face.

Jesse slid his hand over the top of Tina's. Then he leaned forward and hugged her.

—

We stayed a few days at Bonita's place while Jesse rested up and made sure his sister was being looked after. The head nurse encouraged Jesse to make the trip to Boston; she assured him that Meryl wouldn't be released until her physicians were certain she was stable and that social workers would be visiting her daily after that. Jesse knew that if he won, he wouldn't be fighting again until the fall, which would give him plenty of time to get his family into a better home and find himself a permanent manager.

Against Tina's wishes, I called home from Bonita's place. My sister warned me not to mention her operation, not to mention her involvement in Jesse's training, not to mention O'Shea and not to mention her name.

As it turned out, my father wasn't there when I called. Bonita phoned Azalea, so I asked her to let him know that I was thinking about him. She said she would, then reminded me that I had promised to bring Tina back in one piece.

I was happy that Jesse had agreed to fight, because I knew how much help it could bring his family, and I could see how happy it made Tina. I was glad, too, that Bonita and Paul were coming with us this time; his cardiologist had agreed to the trip providing he only watched the fight and did not take any active part in it. Louise wasn't too sure about the whole thing, but Bonita assured her that she wouldn't let him get stressed out. And Jesse needed to conserve his energy; having three drivers was going to make it easier on everyone involved.

"And besides," Paul argued, "you can't keep me locked up forever. If I can't watch the occasional fight, you might as well kill me right now."

So off we went. I was glad when Paul or Jesse was driving because Bonita sat in the back and we talked about things that had nothing to do with boxing and ate ice cream and listened to the radio and hung our feet out the window. But then I made the mistake of telling her all about the Valentines and when we were getting near their place, she insisted on meeting them.

"No way," said Tina, giving me a look that meant "you and your big mouth."

"Oh, come on," Bonita said with a little whine. "I want to see this place. Besides, I have to pay that Walter fellow for the rad. Daddy would be mad at me if I didn't."

"Send him a cheque," suggested my sister.

It took several miles of arguing back and forth, then finally Bonita played the "it's my car so I say where we go" card and, yes, we ended up back at the Valentines.

We weaved our way down that long driveway, honking at the occasional chicken that strutted out. When the house came into sight and we could see the family sitting on that old car seat, I fully expected Ellwood or Dot to call out, "Look! Here come cousin Ellie and cousin Tina!"

They all dashed over when we pulled in. The kids ran around the car and screamed. Dar and Char headed straight for Jesse, Walter headed straight for Brandy and Dot headed straight for Tina. Ellwood starting opening beers. We had to unclamp Tina's hands from the door handle to get her out of the car.

Dot had supper on – it was stew again, and she'd made plenty of it – so she urged us to stay. Paul and Ellwood discussed the crops, the weather and which chickens were the best layers (Rhode Island Reds); Bonita and Walter discussed the life and times of Brandy; and while Tina sulked most of the time, I took some photographs. And when Dot asked Tina if she had that letter for Carson, and Tina lied and said she'd lost it again, and Dot came out with a third one, this time I kept it. Together with my photographs, it would be a way to remember.

Boston was a few hours from the Valentines' place and while we could have made it, Dot insisted we stay the night. This time, Paul slept in the barn with Jesse; Bonita and Tina took the guest room and I stayed on the couch. It meant that I couldn't get any sleep until after *The Tonight Show* was over, but I didn't mind – there were some interesting things stuck in the back of the sofa. I found a tractor manual (with a nude picture from *Playboy* magazine hidden inside), a fishbone, at least two dozen strands of embroidery thread and Dot's cameo brooch that, it turned out, had been missing for seven years.

I sat with Dot while she laughed and ate chips and worked on her needlepoint. It was almost done when she went to bed, so I did the last few stitches for her.

In the middle of the flowers and vines, where I figured there should be a birdhouse or maybe a watering can or something, there was another biblical verse, like the one on the wall. This time it was from the Twenty-third Psalm: "The Lord is my shepherd, I shall not want. He maketh me to lie down in green pastures, He leadeth me beside still waters. He restoreth my soul."

And although I never did see the Valentines again, every time I hear that verse, I think of Dot and her needlepoint – and Johnny Carson.

CHAPTER TWENTY-ONE

Jesse was so focused on the fight, I didn't see much of him for a couple of days after we arrived in Boston. Paul wasn't supposed to be involved in his training whatsoever; he couldn't even remind him to keep his toes pointed in. But whenever Bonita turned her head, he tossed Jesse a piece of advice like bread crumbs to a duck. And if Tina breathed a word that even smelled like pugilism, Bonita cut her off mid sentence. Needless to say, Tina's ire was up to the roof after a few days.

I, on the other hand, loved having Bonita around, not only because she insisted that we stay in a nicer place than the seedy motels we'd been forced to endure, but also because she and I spent time window shopping and enjoying the sights of Boston. Before we left on our excursions, Bonita would make Tina promise not to involve Paul in any boxing-related activities. Making my sister promise anything, though, was like telling a four-year-old not to run her finger along a newly-frosted cake. So every time we headed out the door, Tina and Paul glanced at each other from under their eyelids and swore they wouldn't talk shop.

Boston is a wonderful city, and probably the most historic place in all of America. It's pretty, too. The downtown is located on a peninsula that juts into Boston Harbor, with the Charles River beginning at the north end and flowing past. From the time we arrived, Bonita and I never shut up about the Boston tea party and Paul Revere's ride; Tina and Paul never shut up about the Boston Garden, that famous venue that had hosted The Rolling Stones and The Beatles and Jimi Hendrix and just about every huge sports event in history. We were all excited to think that Jesse would be fighting at the Garden in the fall if he won this next fight.

I was glad that Tina had Jesse's fight to preoccupy her thoughts; I found that even with Bonita and Paul Revere around to take my mind off Count Ilizarov, just knowing the hospital was around the corner left a permanent knot in the centre of my stomach.

Bonita sensed it, and on our last day of sightseeing, when we were having supper alone (Tina was busy with Jesse, and Paul was pretending to rest), she asked me about Tina.

"She's hard-headed," I told Bonita, as if she didn't know already. "I can't talk her out of it."

"Maybe it's the right thing," suggested Bonita.

"I like her the way she is."

"So do I." Bonita picked up a menu and looked it over. With everything looming the way it was – the fight, the hospital – the only thing I could manage was a bowl of soup.

"Did you ever get a hold of your daddy?" Bonita asked me.

"No, not yet."

"Tina really takes after him, doesn't she?" She took a few sips of water. "They both love boxing so much."

"Too much. Neither one of them can imagine life without it."

"It must make her crazy to think about his hand," said Bonita.

"Why?"

"Well, you know…."

"No, I don't know anything."

"Oh. Oh, dear."

I didn't understand what Bonita was getting at. Then I realized she had spilled the beans and was trying to change the topic.

"Are you sure you only want soup?" she hedged. "How about a nice dessert?"

She wasn't going to get around me with pie. Not even cheesecake would get her out of this one.

"Bonita, why would Tina care so much about my father's hand?" I stared her down. "Please, I have to know."

"Oh, me and my great big mouth."

"Come on, tell me."

"I figured that by now you two would have known about it. It's been sixteen years, for heaven's sake."

The waitress gave me my soup and placed a toasted sandwich and salad in front of Bonita. She asked us if we needed anything else, then left.

"So this was when I was a year old and Tina was two?"

"Yes."

And then, realizing the jig was up, Bonita made me cross my heart and hope to die and not say one word to Tina.

When she told me what happened, I almost died anyway.

"He was getting ready for the fight. A couple of jerks made some pretty terrible comments about Tina. About her being a dwarf. I think they called her— well, you know."

"Retarded?"

She looked away for a minute. "Yeah, something like that."

"So my father was defending Tina? That's how he wrecked his fist?"

Bonita nodded. "She was such a pretty little girl. I don't know how they could be so cruel. I just don't." She waved her finger. "But your daddy took them on. He had the two of them by the neck. I think he was going to kill them."

"What happened?"

"Somebody stopped him. Reminded him he had two little girls to look after, and if he went to jail, there'd be no one to care for them."

"So he threw his fist into the wall instead."

"Exactly."

—

I didn't have a chance to digest the news. It was almost time for the fight, so Bonita and I hurried back to the hotel. Jesse was already at the arena, and Paul and Tina were with the promoter. Bonita and I took showers and changed clothes and were ready to leave, when Paul and Tina came barrelling down the hallway.

"I really didn't need this," cried my sister, crashing into our room and throwing herself into a chair.

"Mind if I come in?" asked Paul.

"Not at all," said Bonita. "Come in, come in. What's going on? You're supposed to be resting," she told Paul.

"We've got some, uh, interesting news," he said.

"The guy who Jesse was supposed to fight tonight – the Canadian title holder – well, he's out with an injury, and guess who's taking his place?" hollered Tina.

I shrugged. Bonita shrugged.

"Go on, guess." Tina hollered even louder.

"The Eastern Canadian champion," said Paul. "Flyin' Ryan Byrne."

"Oh, no," I said.

"Oh, yes," Tina said. "How the hell am I supposed to concentrate?"

"Concentrate?" I asked. "What? You're worried about your concentration? What about Dad?"

"Look, Ellie, in two short hours I have to coach Jesse. You're just going to have to keep off my back. This is important to me, okay?"

A tremendous surge of anger swelled up inside and I could hear blood rushing to my ears. I felt sick at my stomach.

How can she hate our father so much? How can she do this to him? Especially after everything he has sacrificed for her!

"Tina," I blurted, "you can't do this to Dad. Don't you know…?"

I glanced at Bonita and she gave me a steely look.

"Don't I know what?" asked Tina.

"Well ... well don't you care about him? How can you go on with the fight now? You can't. I won't let you."

"Like hell I won't."

"Well I won't be there. Dad is depending on Ryan's win. You can't do this."

"Just watch me," said Tina.

"I won't be your cut man," I said sulkily.

"You're a lousy cut man anyway."

Paul broke in. "Come on, girls," he said, "let's let the best man win, shall we?" He smiled, but it didn't work.

"Well, you can coach Jesse then," I said to Paul.

"No, he can't." Bonita was firm.

"Shut up, Ellie," said my sister, "and stay out of it."

"How *can* you?"

She looked at me for a minute. Then she said that I would just have to trust her.

Trust her?

The frustration built up and I wanted to scream, "Dad gave up his whole boxing future for you and you won't even give up one fight for him?"

Instead I marched right over to my sister and hollered at her from less than a foot away.

"You don't have to worry about the Ilizarov procedure damaging your heart," I said, wanting to hurt her. "You don't have one!"

Then I stormed out the door.

CHAPTER TWENTY TWO

I think it was a bus that almost hit me. I was trying to cross in front of the arena. It wasn't the city lights that blinded me, nor the grinding noise of traffic that disoriented me. It was my sister. All I could see in front of me was her – her laughing face and her finger pointing down to the coal mine like the grim reaper. If a cab driver hadn't shouted at me to get the hell out of his way, the reaper would have got me too. I flew through the front door of the arena, showed them my pass and searched frantically for Ryan. I wanted to warn him that Tina was Jesse's coach. Up one hallway, down another – nothing, nothing.

I started to go in circles and wound up at the front entrance again, so I asked directions from the man who had checked my ticket. When I turned to head back down the hall, I ran straight into Mickey O'Shea.

"Hey, kid, ready for the big fight?"

"I thought you didn't have anything riding on this."
Not that I believe a word you say.

"I don't. Just checking out the guy from Edmonton who's fighting Mankiller."

"Nope."

"What do you mean, nope?" he asked me.

"Guy from Edmonton can't fight and Ryan Byrne is filling in for him." I turned to leave.

"Oh," he said. "Mankiller's got that one."

"That's what worries me."

"Why?"

"Because I need Ryan to win."

I left him standing there and tried navigating the next corridor. Finally I came to a dressing room – it was Jesse's. He saw me and came out.

"Ellie," he called, thinking I'd missed the doorway. Then he took a good look at my face. "What's wrong with you?"

"Nothing wrong with me," I declared. "There's lots wrong with Tina, though."

"Is she okay?"

"Oh, sure, she's always fine, isn't she?"

"What's going on?"

"Haven't you heard who you're fighting yet?"

He shook his head. "The promoter said the guy I was supposed to fight had some kind of an injury. They're bringing in a replacement." He walked closer to me. "Why?"

"Ryan Byrne," I replied. "That's who you're going to fight."

Jesse didn't say anything for a full minute.

Then he swore a few times under his breath and sat down on a bench next to the door to his dressing room. He clenched his hands into fists and pounded them into his knees.

"Yup, that's right. Tina wants you to knock the hell out of the only guy on the planet that can keep my father out of the mines."

Still, he said nothing. Just stared into space.

"I begged her not to do this. I know you need the money, Jesse, but you'll get a big share of the purse whether you win or lose. Right?"

Then I heard voices behind me.

It was Ryan Byrne and his manager, a slick looking man with wavy black hair.

"What are *you* doing here?" was Byrne's warm greeting. His gaze went to Jesse and then back to me again. "I guess your sister must be here someplace too."

Tina came around the corner. She had a water bottle, an ice bucket and sponges. And a bag of medicine.

"There she is," I said.

Byrne looked at her and saw the supplies in her arms. "I don't need *your* help," he scoffed. "You never give up, do you?"

Tina ignored him and turned to Jesse.

"Come on," she said, "let's get you taped up." She gave me a dirty look that said "traitor." Then she decided to speak to me. "Are you going to change your mind and help me or do I have to take a cut man provided by the promoter?" I didn't answer her, so she headed into the dressing room.

"What's she talking about? What's she doing?" asked Byrne. "Why is she with Jesse Mankiller?"

Tina stuck her head out the doorway.

"Because I'm Mr. Mankiller's manager."

—

"I gave you your instructions in the dressing room. Remember to protect yourself at all times and above all, obey my commands," said the referee. "Touch 'em up ... good luck."

Ryan came out right at the bell. He tried a couple of jabs but didn't connect. Jesse had no problem keeping away from his uppercuts, but wasn't fighting like he should have been. Didn't have the same fire or energy that he used to. He looked half asleep. I heard Tina tell him to wake up.

Something was wrong.

"Stick and run, stick and run," hollered Byrne's coach.

I was sitting so close to the ring I could almost reach out and touch the red velvet ropes. The arena was packed, and if I was harbouring any glimmer of hope that the event wouldn't be televised, the camera crew that set up near Byrne's corner did away with that notion on the spot. Bonita and Paul were further back, an intentional move on Bonita's part to keep him from yelling instructions at Jesse.

The cut man they'd provided for Jesse was busy getting the enswell ready and Tina was barking at him about when to use Avitene, when to use Adrenaline hydrochloride and when to use her special salve.

Ryan's team was shouting orders too, mostly reminding Byrne to go for the head and snap with a left jab. He was using that trick of not letting on he was a southpaw, but Tina would have warned Jesse before the match. Which made me wonder what the heck was wrong.

Jesse appeared to have lost the very thing that Tina said would take him to the top – the fact that he was both quick and powerful at the same time. And there weren't the usual screams and hollers from the crowd – not yet anyway – mostly because nothing was happening. I think Ryan's team told him to chase Jesse around a bit, throw the odd punch but remain defensive until the second round.

I presumed that Tina had probably given Jesse the same advice; I could see no other reason for his empty-handed performance.

I don't know what was said in the dressing room, but I could hear everything she told him between rounds – I was sitting that close – and it soon became clear that she didn't know what was going on with him.

"Why the hell didn't you take that shot after he threw the left cross? He was wide open."

By the third round, the crowd was becoming its obnoxious self, but somehow above the roar I thought I heard someone call out my name. I scanned the seats and saw Dan Campbell weaving his way from the back of the arena toward me.

"Hey, Ellie," hollered Dan. "I figured you and Tina would be here to watch Ryan. But what's she doing on the other side? What's going on?"

"It's a long story," I said. "We met Jesse along the way but had no idea he'd wind up fighting Ryan." Some men behind us tried to push us out of their line of sight, so Dan found us a spot in the aisle.

"Your father's here, you know. He got word about Ryan yesterday morning, so we drove down."

I buried my face in my hands. "Oh, God."

"So you didn't know? Tina doesn't know he's here?"

"No. And Ryan didn't bother to tell us."

"He didn't bother to get your father a seat, either, the dumb jerk." Dan shook his head in disgust. "After all that training, you'd think he wouldn't leave him standing against the back wall."

The bell rang. Byrne rushed out of his corner and snapped out a powerful left jab into Jesse's forehead, then another into his mouth, then he hurled him against the ropes.

The camera zoomed in for a close look at the blood.

Something was wrong. Even with my paltry knowledge of boxing, I knew that Jesse was a better fighter than that.

Tina knew it too. She was shouting orders like a drill sergeant.

The crowd was on its feet, screaming. Jesse was banged again and again and again and again.

"I heard Mankiller was better than this," said Dan.

"He is."

Slam. Slam. Slam.

Jesse's forehead was torn open and one of his eyes was swelling shut.

Down he went.

The referee rushed in to see if he was fit to carry on. He signalled the doctor, and the two of them looked for signs of disorientation and examined Jesse's pupils for dilation. The doctor nodded to Tina to clean him up.

"What the hell is it?" she said. "If I didn't know better, I'd say you were...." And then it dawned on her. I could see it in her face. "Jesse, you're taking a dive. For God's sake, you're taking a dive. What the hell? What did O'Shea promise you?"

Jesse didn't reply.

"You told me you wouldn't take a dive for anybody," screamed Tina.

Still no reply.

"Mankiller," insisted Tina, "why are you taking a dive? I want an answer and I want it now."

Jesse didn't say a word.

"Answer me!"

But Jesse refused. And then, without warning, he did something that not even the best psychic in Boston could have predicted.

He pushed out his mouthpiece with his tongue, spat into the bucket, put his gloves around my sister's neck, pulled her to his chest and kissed her like I'd never seen anybody be kissed before.

CHAPTER TWENTY-THREE

The crowd went wild. A wave of oohs and aahs rolled across the stadium. The camera crew circled the ring to get a better shot.

I can't believe it. Jesse's taking a dive for Tina.

"He's letting Byrne win – he's doing it for our gym!" I grabbed Dan Campbell's arm, but he was so busy watching Tina be kissed by Jesse, he didn't hear a word I said.

He turned to me. "Him and … Tina?"

"I guess so!" I said. "I've got to find my father. Where is he?"

"I'll get him," offered Dan. Then he dashed to the back of the arena.

When Jesse finally let Tina go, she was so stunned, she stood there like a department store mannequin. It was the ringside physician that brought her back to reality when he said Jesse could continue the fight. I'd hoped he wouldn't. I'd hoped for a technical knockout, because I couldn't stand to watch Jesse take any more abuse.

Then came the biggest surprise of all. This time it came from Tina.

I didn't hear everything she said, because she was talking into Jesse's ear with cupped hands, but I did catch the last line.

"And that's why you have to do everything you can to win this thing. Everything."

The bell rang. Jesse looked at Tina, and she nodded. She sponged him off quickly, then sent him into the ring.

Whatever she whispered to Jesse changed the whole course of the fight, because from that point on, even though he'd allowed himself to take repeated blasts to the face, he came out more powerful than ever.

Oh my God. He's going to kill Ryan.

"Keep on him, Jesse," screamed Tina, "don't let him rest."

What's she doing?

Everything was being drowned out by the shouts from the crowd. The cheers, the boos, the multitude of voices all merged together into one thunderous boom.

With his long braid swinging behind him like a tail, Jesse went after Ryan like a fierce animal after its prey. Across the ring he flew, swinging, slugging and flinging sweat in every direction. Every jab, every cross, hit Ryan in the face, and his blood started to flow. Everything was covered in it – their faces, their gloves, their arms. Tina was yelling, screaming. The crowd was bellowing. Jesse was on automatic pilot, throwing lefts and rights and driving poor Ryan onto the deck.

Crack.

The right connected and Ryan was down.

The referee gave him the count. He got up with two seconds to spare and stumbled around like a drunk. The gash on his cheek was gushing blood like a fireplug.

The physician took him aside and together with the cut man, tried to clean him up.

Jesse waited in the neutral corner.

And then, for some reason known only to her, my sister marched across the ring and handed the physician her jar of salve. He nodded and pushed some into Byrne's wound. It worked like a charm.

"You don't have to thank me," she told Ryan. "I'm just making sure you lose fair and square." He scowled at her, and her blue eyes stared back at him like tiny knives.

I ran up to the ropes.

"Tina! Tina!" I yelled until I got her attention. "Dad's here. DAD'S HERE."

She heard me, but all she said was, "Good."

Good? That's it? Good?

The physician let the fight continue. The ref cleaned off Byrne's gloves and sent him back into the ring, but this time it didn't last long.

Jesse's left arm was pumping out like a machine.

"Keep on him!" shouted my sister. The words that once excited me, made me feel sick to my stomach.

"Stick and move, stick … stick," hollered Byrne's manager but it was too late. Ryan fell to his knees and his gloves hit the canvas. Then he collapsed.

The counting began, "One … two … three …"

Ryan couldn't get up. The crowd went wild. It was over. My sister had accomplished what she'd always wanted to do. She had defeated my father.

Congratulations, Tina. I hope you're happy. If only you knew what he sacrificed for you. If only I hadn't listened to Bonita and told you. Maybe I could have changed your mind.

The referee held up Jesse's right arm. The crowd roared. The ring announcer screamed into the microphone:

"Here is your winner, and the new North American champion – Jesse Mankiller…."

—

Once they'd whisked Ryan Byrne away for treatment and slapped some bandages on Jesse, the emcee prepared the crowd for a big announcement.

"Ladies and … Ladies and gentlemen," he said, waiting for the deafening cheers to settle.

Jesse pushed his stool into the middle of the ring and held Tina's hand while she climbed up on top of it.

"Ladies and gentlemen, Mr. Mankiller's manager has something to say about his upcoming fight." He gave the microphone to Tina.

The camera circled in on my sister. Newspaper journalists raced to the edge of the ring.

I can't watch this, I told myself. I started walking toward the back wall in search of my father. He was heading toward me and we met halfway.

"Ellie!" He grabbed me and gave me a hug. Then he looked up at Tina in the ring. "Thank God she didn't go through with it," he said. "She isn't going to—"

"I don't know, Dad. But look what she's done! She's helped Jesse Mankiller to win. And Ryan to lose!"

"I'll figure something out for us," said my father. "I just want you two to come home, okay?"

Tina's voice reverberated throughout the building as she spoke into the microphone.

"As you all know," she said, "in September, Mr. Mankiller will be fighting here in Boston for the world title."

The crowd roared.

"And …" She waited a few seconds. "And he has asked me to announce the name of his permanent manager."

Permanent manager?

I looked at Dad, and he shrugged.

"If he will accept the position, Mr. Mankiller feels the best man for the job – the only man for the job – is my father, Sandy MacKenzie."

The journalists started popping questions. Tina over-rode them all.

"A former world-class boxer, Sandy MacKenzie now trains many fine athletes from his gym in Sydney, Cape Breton. I understand he's in the house tonight…."

The lights started dancing and circling the arena, trying to find my father.

"Dad!" I hollered over the booming applause. "You're going to be – you're going to be Jesse's manager!" He was stunned – we both were – and I nudged him into the aisle. Then I lifted my father's arm into the air and called out, "Here he is! Here's Sandy MacKenzie!"

The spotlight followed him as he made his way to the ring, and Jesse lifted the rope for him to duck underneath. Then the two of them shook hands.

If I hadn't known better, I would have sworn there were tears in my dad's eyes. I couldn't tell, because there were too many in my own.

And then I understood. I understood everything.

Tina knew Ryan Byrne wasn't going to make it to the top; he'd never save our gym. She knew that Jesse would be the one to go the distance. She knew that he'd be the one to keep our father out of the mines.

—

Bonita and Paul pushed through the crowd until they found us, and Dan wasn't far behind. Tina and I were standing in the corridor near the ring, and my father was in the dressing room with Jesse. Paul congratulated Tina, then hurried off to see Jesse.

"And you said men weren't interested in you," teased Bonita. Then she hugged my sister.

"Great about your dad," said Dan. "He deserves this."

"He certainly does," said Bonita. "So what happens now?" she asked Tina. "Are you—"

"I'm not going to the hospital, if that's what you want to know," Tina said. "Except to talk to Dr. Campbell and thank him."

"You're not?" asked Dan. "It's such a good—"

"I've given this a lot of thought over the last few weeks, and – well, I've decided to let someone else have my place in the trial. Someone who can really use the help."

"But it's—"

"I don't need the operation," said Tina.

The dressing room door swung open, and my father came out smiling. Behind him was Paul, and then came Jesse, looking as gorgeous as ever.

I'm sure that Dan and Bonita thought he was the reason why Tina didn't need the operation anymore. But I knew better. I knew she never needed it in the first place.

EPILOGUE

Tina went back to high school. Back to Steinbeck and *Cannery Row* and all the things she couldn't stand. She completed her courses and even went on to college. My father trained and managed Jesse and, with some help from Tina and her salve, he won the world title and defended it many times.

I haven't seen Jesse in years; Bonita told me he bought a nice place in Truro for his family and that Meryl had turned her life around completely. And she heard that he'd married a young woman from Oklahoma.

Tina's married now too. But I know that she often thinks about the summer of 1979 and our trip to Boston. And Jesse. I am sure she thinks about him.

I became a teacher, and it was when I was moving from Sydney to Halifax that I came across the letter Dot had written to Johnny Carson. Tina and I opened it together.

Dear Johnny,

My name is Dot Valentine. You might remember me as Dorothy Dean. We met thirty years ago, in 1949, in Bar Harbor, Maine. I was eighteen at the time, and you weren't much older yourself.

We spent a lot of time together and I've never had such fun, before or since. I still live in Maine, have seven children and not much else, but I haven't missed your show once since it went on the air.

When a visitor came along this summer, Tina is her name, I knew it was my chance to get this letter directly to you. I've tried mailing letters many times, and have received fourteen autographed photos from members of your staff, but have been unable to reach you personally, to say hello and wish you well.

I hope you remember me.

God bless,

Dorothy (Dean) Valentine

It took several calls, but we finally got through to Mr. Carson and read the letter to him. He did remember Dot and even said hello to her on his program, not long before he retired.

I asked Tina if she thought Dot was watching. She said she didn't care, but by the look on her face, I could tell she really did.

The research and writing of this novel benefitted by support of an Ontario Arts Council Writers' Works in Progress grant.

Many thanks to a fine editor, Marianne Ward, for her invaluable contributions, and to Paul Mac-Dougall, author of *Distinction Earned: Cape Breton's Boxing Legends 1946-1970* (CBU Press).

Caroline Stellings

Caroline is an award-winning author and illustrator of books for children and young adults, including the best-selling Malagawatch Mice series from CBU Press. Her novel *The Contest* (Second Story Press) won the ForeWord Book of the Year Award and, along with *The Malagawatch Mice and the Cat Who Discovered America* (CBU Press), was a finalist for the Hackmatack Children's Choice award. Caroline lives in Waterdown, Ontario.

Also published by CBU Press:

The Malagawatch Mice and the Church that Sailed Skippers Save the Stone /
　　　Na Sgiobairean agus an Lia-Fàil
Around the Year with the Malagawatch Mice /
　　　Feadh na Bliadhna Comhla ri Luchain Mhalagawatch